Steve lives in Somerset with his wife, three grown up children, and big boy Max. He has been working as an Optician for over 40 years.

For Max and Ted

Steve Bennett

MY KIND

AUSTIN MACAULEY PUBLISHERS™

LONDON • CAMBRIDGE • NEW YORK • SHARJAH

A CIP catalogue record for this title is available from the British Library.

ISBN 9781035801800 (Paperback)
ISBN 9781035801817 (ePub e-book)

www.austinmacauley.com

First Published 2023
Austin Macauley Publishers Ltd®
1 Canada Square
Canary Wharf
London
E14 5AA

Table of Contents

Manufactured Beginnings

One of the earliest recollections I have of something 'strange' happening was at elementary school. I must have been around 6 years old and attending the last day of term Christmas party. The teacher had organised 'Pin the tail on the Donkey', which in the States they call 'The Donkey Game', and I was called forward to have a go.

I held the tail in my right hand as the blindfold was fitted over my eyes. I was aware of being able to see the floor as it wasn't a great fit, but otherwise, I could not see anything.

"Come on then, Jamie, let's see how close you can get," said the teacher.

And there it was, as clear as day, like a light switch had been turned on. I could see the picture of the donkey and my hand reaching out with the tail. I stopped and withdrew my right hand and instinctively put my left hand up to the blindfold. Yes, it was still there, I could feel it, and it was completely covering my forward sight, but I could 'see' in my mind's eye.

And because I hesitated, the teacher urged, "Come on…you can do it."

Yes, I most certainly COULD.

I could place the tail perfectly and win!

But I did not.

Even at this early age, something stopped me from even hinting my abilities and I pushed the tail into the donkey's neck.

I was born in America and spent most of my early youth there. My parents were both English but were living in the States due to my father's work commitments. He advised companies on how to improve their cash flow. A business consultant I think was his job title, though I never knew that much about it. My mother was a housewife and brought me up 'the English way.' I can remember her airing her distaste of the American accent that I was acquiring, and some of the slang that I was using, on many occasions, although she always said it in a light humorous fashion.

I knew I was different.

I found learning easy. In fact, sometimes I knew things that I couldn't understand HOW I knew.

Some facts and answers to problems were just there in my head. It was instant. But I did notice, even at this early age, that my abilities didn't remain for long and would alter. The 'seeing through the blindfold' for example, was a one off as far as I can remember.

My parents were always supportive; constantly reassuring me of my self-belief with reminders to always be aware of people around me at all times.

"An unintentional demonstration of your mental skill could lead to all sorts of problems," my father would say, or words to that effect.

I understood, but I found it difficult at times to comply.

In early 1964, when I was about 8 years old, we did the BIG move and 'crossed the pond' to the UK and settled in a place called Hoddesdon in the county of Hertfordshire. I use the word 'settled' rather loosely as it seemed that we were moving house all the time. Over the space of 3 years or so, we must have 'moved' about 4 times, and on each occasion I had to start all over again in the friends' stakes and of course with schooling. It was awkward in many ways. Each time I was the new boy in class. I had an American twang to my accent (sorry mum) and to top that I could do things the others couldn't do mentally. The abilities kept changing though and I became aware of new skills subconsciously. I was being 'informed' somehow directly into my mind. It would just happen. I could be riding my bike, or playing in the street and I would suddenly know.

One example of this was when I was doing homework one evening sitting at the dining table. I picked up my glass of orange squash to have a drink...and the thought arrived. I looked at my pencil sharpener and I knew I could move it without touching it. And I did...straight away. I moved it a few inches. Then I remember looking over my shoulder quickly to see whether one of my parents had noticed.

Around the age of 14 to 15, I decided to write a daily diary.

I wrote the entries in a particular way so that only I could interpret the real meanings. I would write down what I had done, what I had experienced and some of my feelings. But I did it in a certain way that only made sense to me, ensuring that it would be nothing out of the ordinary to a chance reader. I loved reading it back to myself. It made me feel good. I knew it was special, and it allowed me to relive certain 'different' happenings and also to think about the normal events in my life and how I had reacted and dealt with them too.

It was while reading this diary one day, about a month into the recordings, when things suddenly took a rather bizarre turn. I was 'going over' the previous day's entry before writing something new, when I suddenly realised that it had gradually developed into an experience that I had no recollection of at all!

I read it back. It started off quite normally but then it turned into an account that had no connection with my existing life whatsoever. It was like I had slid into someone else's memoirs instead.

It was in my handwriting, but the general expressions and certain wordings were most definitely not from me!

During the following month this happened again two more times. I would be reading the entry from the day before when it started to transform into an experience that I knew nothing about. It was all quite a bit scary at first but after a while it turned into more of a fascination. I would scan the relevant print, paying close attention to each word, looking for a clue. The expression 'reading between the lines' was very relevant as I tried to make some sort of sense of it all. I never told my parents. I knew that it was something that was just pertaining to me and the way that I was different. I cannot explain that properly, I just knew, and so I kept it to myself.

I continued to write the diary for the rest of the year but no more curious items occurred again. I would often sit down and read bits of it back, expecting it to have altered or to have new additions, but it never did. It was just those three times. It was so odd, so weird, and so unexplainable.

I named the diary 'Magical Memories,' and I treated it like it was a wizard's spell book. Every time I opened it, I really believed I was going to read something mystical, and to me I did anyway with the indefinable three entries that were already there at the beginning of the year.

But I wanted more. I wanted new unexplainable listings to happen again, and the diary unfortunately did become quite an obsession. When I was at home I would flick through the pages, reading it over and over, almost willing some unfamiliar sentence to appear.

But gradually over time, this consuming desire waned as nothing out of the ordinary ever came to light again, and soon even my normal daily entries dwindled and became quite infrequent, until finally the want to write anything at all became a thing of the past.

I had a really special bond with my parents and not just because they were my mother and father. They were my advisers, almost life advisers, and they did it in a very low key, inconspicuous way. They 'quietly guided' me, that's the best way to describe it, though it was a natural feeling for me to hide any developing ability from them. I don't know why I did this as I knew that they both were very much aware anyway…especially my father for some reason. It was strange I suppose, not discussing it or explaining anything much, but that's the way it was.

During my teenage schooling days, my peers would often make me conscious of certain oddities and incongruities that were being perceived. But thankfully the nonsensical side of the unexplainable gave light to humour rather than creating disconcerting troublesome attention.

At parent teacher school meetings, certain episodes or particular incidents in class would be brought to light. It was difficult for mum and dad, because the attention varied from one of amazement and praise for my exam results and knowledge in class, to one of bewilderment and puzzlement if I occasionally did something 'odd.' The moving of very light objects was fun. I was very careful at school, occasionally turning it into a 'magic' trick, receiving comments such as, "we know how you're doing that," which was good…because they didn't!

I remember one time when the maths teacher, Mrs Madigan, was chalking a long multiplication equation on the blackboard, and for fun wanted to see who could work out the answer the quickest. I stupidly said the resultant figure as soon as she'd chalked the last bit, to which she said, "that's ridiculous!" as she glanced down at her pre-written solution.

I know I should've kept quiet, but sometimes the answer would just suddenly appear in my mind. I wouldn't even be consciously thinking about it, and I would automatically say it.

I know this WAS advertising my abilities, but occasionally it was very difficult not to.

I remember another phase I went through in my teens where, if someone annoyed me or upset me and I took a dislike to that person, I would hear through a third party that something untoward had happened to them. Thankfully it was nothing too unpleasant and it only happened a few times as I'm pretty easy going and get on with most people. At first I put it down to being just a coincidence, but I knew it was my subconscious acting on it somehow.

The most serious episode during this phase was when I was dating a girl and her ex-boyfriend made it quite clear that he didn't approve. Now, I know I most definitely did not like this chap and I consciously wanted the situation to be easier for me. On this occasion it was deliberate and perceptible. I wanted something to happen to him…and it did. He crashed his motorbike and broke his leg…and he was out of 'circulation' for some time. I was pleased when this ability disappeared. It made me too conscious of my thought patterns, wondering whether I was going to bring harm to someone unintentionally.

My mother and father always handled everything really well and deflected much of the attention the best they could. In today's world, it would have been a different story. I probably would have been diagnosed with some kind of mental health issue, and to be honest it probably would have been much easier and simpler to deal with it all. I would have been labelled and accepted, and everyone would 'understand'.

But I knew that I didn't have an impediment. I knew it was so much more. I felt it was something very special, something that I may use for a purpose and that it was developing and changing for a reason…but I didn't know why, and I didn't think my parents really knew either.

Youthful Move

Around the age of 20 I moved out of my parents' home and I took a courier job in London. I knew I could have applied for most high flying jobs and made a name for myself, but low key, easy going employment, was all I wanted.

I rented an old flat near the depot which certainly made getting out of bed at the last minute rather habit forming. My social life had reduced in volume now as I did not know anyone in the area and for some time I hadn't had any strange or odd mind revelations. The 'moving of objects' lasted for about a year and then I suddenly realised I couldn't do it anymore. It was almost an annoying feeling losing that ability as I did enjoy it, but I somehow knew that a process was taking place in my brain and I just had to accept it.

I had two close friends who would come and visit occasionally but they seemed to be getting busier in their own jobs and with their own commitments and these visits became few and far between.

But this didn't bother me, I enjoyed my own company, and I spent much of it working on an old Suzuki 250cc motorbike that I kept in a nearby garage/room. My father had sourced the bike for me, but it did need a lot of work done to bring it back to its former glory. But this was fine from my point of view. I liked to have a project on the go, something to occupy my mind, and the motorbike fitted the bill. As soon as I turned on the room light, switched on the radio and shut the door, I felt away from the world and all its worries, and this I liked. I would often bring over a mug of tea after work and stand there staring at the bike, just thinking. The bike room was my temple of thought, a place to unwind and relax, even though I was truly working hard to get the thing up and running.

And it was at one of these evenings when something strange took place again.

I was on my knees, cloth in hand, polishing away on the rear wheel rim. The radio was on and my thoughts were of nothing in particular as I furiously rubbed at the brightening metal.

Suddenly, the radio went completely quiet. Startled, I quickly looked up to view the device, but I did not see it. Instead I saw the bike as if I was standing in the doorway of the room, and it wasn't my bike either…it was a different model.

My vision wandered quickly around. There were a lot of shelves and boxes, a stack of books on a table and a washing machine. Things looked different, things WERE different.

THEN suddenly…I WAS looking at the radio. I was back on my knees again and looking at the radio!

I was staring at it and it was playing music…I could hear it.

I immediately got up and went over and turned the music off. Then I looked back at the bike, and it WAS my bike. I looked around the room; everything was back to normal.

17

That was so strange, so different, and I thought about it for ages afterwards. The many various questions that I asked myself gave many various possible answers. But the one thing that I did know for sure was that my mind abilities were altering again.

Known in Scotland

My parents took early retirement just after my 21st birthday and they moved up to Scotland and settled in a newly built bungalow in a small village near the town of Lockerbie.

I would go up to visit them occasionally at weekends, leaving around 2 a.m. on a Saturday morning to arrive there for breakfast. I would spend the day with them, and then travel back early on Sunday morning. It was always a rush doing it this way, but with my work commitments it was the only way I could do it.

My father suggested that I take some holiday and stay a few days with them instead of "all this rushing around over a weekend." I knew it was my mother worrying about me 'falling asleep at the wheel' really, but it did sound like a good idea and so I arranged with work to get some time off and planned it for a couple of months ahead.

I still left in the early hours of Saturday morning for the journey. It was so good doing it this way as the roads were practically clear all the way and it made a nice easy, stress free, drive up.

As per normal, my mother cooked me a fried breakfast when I arrived and the three of us spent the day chatting and reminiscing.

During the conversation my father spoke about his house insurance and how he wished he had never changed companies when they came up here.

In England, our house was insured with Royal London, and Arthur, my father, felt he was almost coerced into changing to a Scottish company by the builder.

He got some of his 'southern' paperwork out as he was talking, and I noticed an old Royal London bookmark type card with a list of the company office addresses on it, and one of them was in Dumfries, which was only just a few miles away.

"Hey, as I'm staying a few days, why don't we go there on Monday morning and we could change the insurance over," I said with a 'light bulb type moment' tone to my voice.

My mother, Jane, gave a welcoming smile as she exchanged a knowing glance with my father. "That's a good idea, thank you Jamie, your father would appreciate that I'm sure…now…who wants a cup of tea?"

Sunday eased by. We spent most of it chatting in the living room with my mother providing a constant supply of tea and biscuits. I loved this, and it brought back memories of us all living together in the 'good old days.'

Before we retired for the evening, my father mentioned that his back was playing up again. He'd 'niggled' it whilst gardening the other day and was not sure whether we should delay the trip to Dumfries for another time.

"Let's see how you feel in the morning," I said, "and if you're not up to it I can go anyway and try and get it sorted out by myself if you like?"

I could tell that he did 'like', and I reassured him that I'd go in the morning if he wasn't feeling right.

Unfortunately the next day, his back hadn't improved and he said that he'd better not risk travelling, and suggested that I go if I was still keen…but on one condition that we all had lunch together first. I agreed, and we all sat down to eat just after 1.00 p.m.

I had my father's old road map of the area and after a little bit of stop-starting, I found the place. It was a big old country house that had been converted into business offices. It was all painted white, with a long winding drive which led up to a grand set of steps that preceded the doorway into the building.

As I turned off the engine I immediately noticed a few cars that were parked nearby.

There was a Ford Anglia, a Rover 2000 and a Morris Minor…crikey, it was like a gathering of 'old bangers,' and they all looked in pretty good condition too. And knowing my father's love for old cars, I was thinking how he would be reacting if he could see all this.

I looked over to the steps and saw a sign that appeared to have company names printed upon it. I got out of the car and walked over, and noticed that 'Royal London' was one of them.

As I started to walk up the steps, a rather tall lady was coming down.

"Morning," I said, greeting her with my normal cheery voice. She walked straight past, not a nod or a word spoken in response. She didn't even look up to engage eye contact! How rude, and my father always says how unfriendly the people are in London compared with the Scots! Hmmm.

I continued up the steps to the top, opened the door, and went inside, to be met by a large open hallway with a superb ornate central staircase that swept upwards to the other floors. Either side of this were numerous doors with the different names of the many businesses upon them.

I walked to the left side of the stairs, looking at the words printed on the various glass windows, when I suddenly caught my foot and stumbled forward. I looked back to see a raised bit of floor tile, then I looked up to see if anyone had noticed my misfortune. There was no one to be seen. I smiled because I'd made quite a loud noise when I fell forward. My foot had smacked the hard floor in an effort to regain balance and it had echoed down the hall. I regained composure and looked up at the door in front of me, and there it was, the Royal London office. I smiled again as I knocked on the door and turned the brass knob handle to enter. It was stuck, no…it was locked. I cupped my hands to the glass pane and peered through the semi-frosted window. I could just make out some desks and filing cabinets but no people. I took a step back and then noticed the printed opening hours…

'Closed Monday.'

…and then I had that feeling that we all get sometimes, when we suddenly realise that what we've been doing has been a total waste of time!

I looked to the heavens as if for inspiration then turned and walked back through the hallway and down the steps to my car.

There wasn't a soul around, well, other than that woman, but she was now long gone. I hesitated and looked back up at the entrance. Perhaps I should go and try a few of the other doors…but what was the point? The Royal London office was closed anyway.

I looked at the old cars again for a moment and then drove back to my parents' house.

"Well, at least we know where they are," said my mother trying to make me feel better, as she poured out a cup of tea.

"Why don't we try again tomorrow…and I'll come with you this time," added my father, "I'm sure my back will feel better by then."

The next morning my father walked into the kitchen for breakfast wearing a shirt and tie. That was a dead giveaway for me. Whenever he went to work or whenever he went out, he would always wear a tie. He loved to look smart, and he had quite an assortment of designs too. "One for every colour of the rainbow," he always used to say.

He was still not feeling 100%, but he insisted on going and we left just after 9 a.m.

I'd mentioned the old cars that I'd seen yesterday and as we drove up the long twisty drive towards the big white building, I reminded my father of the superb sight he was about to experience.

The large steps came into sight and there was a free car parking space right in front of them. I commented straight away that it looked a lot busier than yesterday as the car park was almost full.

"I don't believe it," I said as I scanned the immediate area… "Sorry dad…there's not one old banger anywhere!"

We got out of the car and I immediately looked across for the sign.

"That's strange, it's gone."

My father looked at me puzzled.

"The Business sign with Royal London on it…" I continued, pointing with my finger. "It was there yesterday, but gone today…"

I scanned the area. Things looked different. It was an odd feeling.

I glanced back at my father who had already started to climb the steps…but rather cautiously.

"Are you going to be alright?" I asked.

"Yes, yes, come on…I'll be fine," he replied.

I scooted past him and kept 3 or 4 steps ahead as I looked back to make sure that he was going to be OK. When we got to the top I held the door open to let him through and we went inside.

I then stopped dead in my tracks.

Things definitely looked different.

Things sounded different too.

I looked down at the carpet and did an exaggerated walking action, "Wow, they got this fitted quick," I said as I pointed and explained the comment to my father. I then looked around at the general interior. "It looks like they've had an overnight refit." I exclaimed.

A lady then suddenly appeared from behind a desk. She was dressed very smartly in a dark blue two-piece jacket and skirt with an orange silk scarf draped around her neck. "Good morning, may I help you both?" she enquired. "Good morning to you," I replied, looking around. "No, it's fine thanks, we're just here to have a word with someone about insurance," as I pointed further down the hallway.

"Insurance?" said the woman in a puzzled voice, "ah, hold on, are you here to see Mr Johnson?" Without waiting for my reply she continued, "Please take a seat I'll tell him you're here."

She motioned with her hand towards a line of chairs against the wall, and then she walked away.

I mischievously smiled at my father who was pulling a face of uncertainty at me, but we walked over to the seats nevertheless and sat down.

"What are we doing?" said my father as he gave me one of his 'looks'.

"Oh come on, let's see where it goes," I responded. "As long as they're from Royal London it doesn't matter who we talk to really, does it?…"

A short, stocky looking, balding man, wearing black trousers and a white shirt came walking towards us…

"Good morning, that was rather quick," he said as he offered his hand to us both rather eagerly, "Come this way do," he added as he turned, fiddling with his low slung tie.

I knew this was a misunderstanding but I wanted to go along with it. I love situations like this when you know what's going on but the other party doesn't. Most people would've stopped it all by now, including my father if he'd been on his own, but that was not me. It wasn't life or death, and besides, I wanted to see how far this would go. I like to play the 'acting ignorant' card now and then; perhaps it's a control thing. In fact it probably is. I've always liked to have the upper hand without anyone else knowing that I did. A mechanic friend of mine once fitted an old Fiat/Ferrari engine into an ageing Ford Capri that I had, and then I drove around knowing that other drivers were unaware of the immense power that lay beneath the bonnet. I loved it. The secret power was there if I wanted to use it, and sometimes I did. I would never brag about it. I just knew that I had the ace if I ever wanted to play it...

I felt my father tugging on my shirt from behind as we all walked into the office. I glanced back with a knowing smile and a nod of my head.

"Please have a seat," said Mr Johnson as he sat himself down in his plush black leather chair behind a rather large oak desk.

My father spoke with a deliberate laugh in his voice as he couldn't contain himself any longer. "I have a feeling that you think we're both someone that we're not," he said as he glanced at me with the look that says 'enough is enough.' He then went to great lengths explaining the reason why. This was my father all over, he never got straight to the point; he always went 'around the houses'. Tongue in cheek, I always blamed him for me not getting better grades in English Literature at school because I always felt I had inherited his poor summarising techniques.

Mr Johnson listened as I joined in too, elaborating further on my experience yesterday with a tone almost bordering on complaint I guess, though I didn't mean it to be that way.

"...and who closes on a Monday anyway...the week's only just started for goodness sake!" I finished off...with a slight laugh in my voice.

There was a long pause as the man behind the desk slowly leaned back in his chair, exhaling loudly as he did so.

"Well, thank you for that", he said with a smile on his face. Mr Johnson was a serious business man, but he also had a great sense of humour and a good understanding of people. That's what he always told his wife anyway.

He leaned forward, "Well, let me tell you two things."

"One, we work here Monday to Friday. Saturday and Sunday is WHEN we're closed…and TWO, Royal London Insurance used to rent an office here many moons ago, and I know that because my uncle used to work for them, but like I say, that was many years ago, and I don't know where their offices are now…but they are certainly not here!"

I looked at my father quickly then back at Mr Johnson. "I was here yesterday, well, not exactly here, it was an office further down the hallway. I tried to open the door, then realised that they were closed…the sign said Royal London, I know it did…" I was talking quite quickly, the mischievous tones were gone, as my confused mind was now trying to fathom out what was being said. Arthur calmly intervened, "Could we have a quick look," he said in a hopeful but knowing sort of tone, as he pointed to the door.

"Yes, of course," replied Mr Johnson. He could tell I was getting a bit anxious, and I most certainly was.

He stood up swiftly and walked out into the hallway. I followed, striding with purpose. I was intent on finding the Royal London office door as I walked past him and further down the hall. "It's here I think," I said as I gesticulated with my hand.

My father came over to me, deliberately blocking Mr Johnson's view of my face, "Are you sure we've got the right place?" He said in a soft definite tone.

I stared at him. It was the kind of stare that said a lot without saying anything if you know what I mean.

Then Mr Johnson walked over to us and pointed at the door, "You're right, this was the old Royal London office, but they haven't been here since, ooooh…probably the late 60s."

I glanced through the window. I could see many people sitting at desks using telephones. "Who are these people then, who do they work for?" I asked annoyingly.

"They work for me," replied Mr Johnson with a laugh in his voice, "this place is my business...we're a marketing company."

I looked at him then back through the glass at the people.

"Oh god, this is crazy; I was here, I was standing here yesterday" ...then I remembered, "Ah yes, hold on...what about the carpet?" I asked the question rather rapidly in my futile attempt to try and hang on to any kind of sensibility in my head, as I quickly turned back to him. "This must have been fitted last night, because this wasn't here yesterday!"

I was getting more and more perturbed and the volume of my voice had increased. The lady on the reception desk reacted and walked over. "Is everything OK Mr Johnson?"

"Yes, no worries Sue...we've just got a little bit of confusion here."

The two exchanged knowing looks and she turned and walked back to the front of the hallway.

My father reassuringly tapped my arm. "Come on, let's get back to the car...we can talk outside."

"Well, what about the carpet then?" I said, ignoring my father and looking again at Mr Johnson.

"Well, it was definitely here yesterday," he replied with a wry smile. "It's about two years old I suppose but still looking fairly good considering the amount of feet that walk upon it every day."

I felt really odd as I hesitated for a moment, and then I looked at my father.

"Come on…" he said again as he made a move towards leaving.

Mr Johnson walked with us to the front entrance.

"I'm not sure what's going on but I hope you get it sorted out," he said rather loudly behind us as we made our way down the steps to the car.

I got in the car, shut the door, and stared straight ahead. Then I turned to my father who had just sat down gingerly in the passenger seat.

"Honest dad, I know this all sounds mad, but I was here yesterday, and everything was different, it really was."

Arthur looked deep in thought as he too stared straight ahead.

"Dad?" I said as I queried my father's lack of response, watching him continue to gaze into space. Then he slowly turned his head, looked at me, and opened his mouth as if to talk, then paused.

"Dad…what's wrong?"

He looked at me for a few more seconds…

"No, there's nothing wrong boy, come on…let's get back home."

I knew now that there WAS something wrong as my father only ever called me 'boy' when he was being serious or had something on his mind. I knew my father's idiosyncrasies too well.

I started the car.

"Look, I'm sorry dad; I don't know what else to say. It's just…so weird."

"Don't worry, come on, drive us back…don't worry."

I could really tell that he was holding out on me, and there was a strained silence on the return journey to the house.

"How did you get on?" Said my mother as she poured out some tea. She would almost always have drinks or a meal ready for my father when he'd been out somewhere. She would wait by the front window looking up the road, and then once she had caught a glimpse of his car coming around the corner she would almost run to the kitchen, and I knew she had done it this time too.

"Speak to dad," I replied as I walked past her on the way to the toilet.

When I re-emerged, I was met with a continuation of my father's non expressive self, though I knew that they had both been talking. When we sat down and had our tea; he spoke to me the most I think he'd ever done about my ability, and described my experience yesterday as mind travel. He said that my hidden consciousness had visited another time and place and that I had 'lived' it in images that my mind had created. I sort of understood what he was saying, but I said that I felt that I was physically there. He smiled and said what he always said when he didn't want to say any more…

"The mind is the universe, Jamie…the mind is the universe."

Improbable Crash

It was now just after my 22nd birthday, and I had finally finished the motorbike project which pleased me immensely. I was still working as a courier driver and had formed a friendship with a chap who I regularly delivered parcels to. Dave had long dark scraggy shoulder length hair, was around 6 foot tall, medium build and always seemed to be wearing a dark sweatshirt and blue jeans. He was a few years older than me, a bit of a wise guy I suppose, but I liked his sense of humour and we had the same shared interest in motorbikes. He had an old blue Suzuki GT750 which he had recently renovated too, and at one of these 'delivery' meetings he suggested we 'air' our machines at the weekend and meet up for a drink. I agreed and met Dave at a biker's type pub on Saturday night and was introduced to one of his friends called Dan. He was a tall, slim chap, with well-groomed short black hair and with eyes that reminded me of an Egyptian Pharaoh as they were dark, long, and slightly slanted…and very striking. He wore black close fitting jeans, a white round collarless long sleeved shirt and a black waistcoat. He came across as a nice lad but every now and then it seemed like he wasn't completely focused on the conversation. I always felt I could tell what someone was like after being with them for a few minutes or so. I did that with Dave. I knew that he was a 'good guy' almost immediately. But with Dan, I wasn't convinced. Sure, he was talking and laughing with Dave and myself, but every now and then it just seemed like he wasn't in the same room so to speak. There's nothing wrong with that of course, for he may have had something on his mind. But there was something else…I just had the feeling.

He went to the toilet at one stage and Dave commented as he sipped his beer, "he's alright is old Danny…"

I nodded my head and then asked, "How long have you known him?"

"I'd say about the same time as I've known you. I met him here. He was new to the area and we just started chatting. He's got his funny ways…like we all have…but he's OK."

I smiled as I took a sip of my drink.

Dan returned and we drank and chatted through to closing time and then we walked outside to our bikes. He'd never mentioned his machine and to be honest he came across as someone who would drive a car rather than ride a motorbike, and I was intrigued to see what it would be. There were 4 bikes parked up, 'leaning in' to each other, that I'd noticed when I arrived, and one of them was a rather dirty Suzuki GT380. Amazingly, this was Dan's! It was a chalk and cheese moment; the mud splattered dirty machine just didn't look right being associated with him.

He started to walk around my bike; his eyes seemingly absorbing every refurbished detail…

"I cannot believe how bloody clean your bike is!" he suddenly said as he turned and looked directly into my eyes.

"Yours would look good too with a bit of spit and polish," I quickly retorted.

"Nah, I just like to ride 'em…hey…come on; let's go for a burn up!"

It was sudden and immediate and he was already fastening the strap of his helmet and walking over to his bike; not waiting for any response from us.

I felt very odd. It was the situation…and a strange feeling swept over me. It stopped me in my tracks as I analysed my thoughts. I think it was a déjà vu moment and I must have looked completely vacant as I glanced over at Dave, but he was being sucked along with Dan's exuberance and he had already started his bike and was turning towards the road.

I still hesitated trying to collect my thoughts as to why I felt this way, but my subconscious was on autopilot and had started my bike…and as I 'refocused,' the three of us accelerated away.

Danny was way ahead, smoke pouring from his three exhausts as he powered up the road with the two of us in hot pursuit. I was wary that I hadn't 'pushed' my machine since the rebuild but the excitement was taking over as I leaned further forward and opened the throttle more to overtake Dave.

I looked quickly in the mirror to check his reaction to my bravado and instantly saw other motorbike lights travelling behind as well. I glanced over my shoulder to view them but they were already level, and three of them powered on by me. One of them brushed against the side of my leg, it was that close. I reacted with an uncharacteristic blaspheme then glanced quickly over my shoulder again as another bike light appeared and immediately shot past me.

I was so pumped up, all rational thoughts had expired. I just now wanted to go faster. I wanted to keep up with them;

I wanted to go with them, to be with them, to be part of the gang. And they were a gang weren't they? I needed to catch them, come on…faster faster…then suddenly…

I WAS with them; I braked hard! I was going to crash! It was right in front of me, I can't avoid it!

"Noooooooo!"

My bike skidded and weaved as the tyres clawed desperately at the road surface, my right hand squeezing, my right foot pushing, as juddering and shaking, and in a screeching cloud of smoke, I came to a thankful upright halt, but at an angle to the curb!

I sat motionless.

My heart was pounding as the sickening smell of burning rubber filled my nostrils.

It was horrible. I saw it, I lived it…I had to crash, there was no avoiding it…I must have crashed.

…But…I didn't…I was alright.

And where were the other bikes? I was with them…but now they're gone.

A car went past beeping its horn in probable reaction to my rather hasty stopping procedure.

Then the distinctive sound of Dave's GT 750 pulled up alongside me.

He flicked up his visor. "For fuck's sake! What are you doing? Why did you DO that? What's wrong…?"

I only half heard what he said as I pushed up my visor too. My mind was racing, trying to fathom out what had just happened…

"…sorry Dave…I'm going to call it a night, going to head back."

"Yeah, alright, but why did you bloody stop like that…Christ, I thought you were going to come off! Are you alright?"

I wasn't alright, I was feeling rather shaken up and I could hear the panic and annoyance in Dave's voice but I didn't want to elaborate, I just wanted to get home.

"Yeah, yeah, I'm fine…sorry, I just wanna get back," and I put the bike into first gear…

"OK mate, well just take it easy…you go on, I'll follow you…and God knows where Danny's got to!"

When I got back home I lay down on the bed with my hands behind my head.

My thoughts were fully centralised on what had happened. I knew that something would occur again, but this one was scary, this one was dangerous, and it all happened too quickly, I had no warning, no time to think. The bike had just appeared, laying there on its side in the road in front of me. I must have hit it…I couldn't avoid it. If it had been further away, I would've had time to swerve, but it was too close, it was just there immediately in front. I had no time to take action. I hit it, I know I did…I felt that I did!

I was reliving it all again in my mind. It was so real. It WAS real. I was there.

I thought back to last year when I tried to visit the Royal London insurance office for my father and what he'd said afterwards. Was that it again? … The hidden subconscious forming images that I had lived? Because Dave didn't experience any of it, it was only me.

In both the Dumfries incident and this one, there was no dividing line between real-time and the event. It all blended together.

And that is what frustrated me when I thought about it, and that I did for quite a while afterwards. It all just happens. But can I influence the situation? Can I actually change things by my actions, or is it all set in stone and I just experience it?

I like to think logically about things, and when it's not logical I get exasperated. I always like to be in control of the situation that I am in. I like to be able to foresee the outcome and plan ahead so to speak. In Dumfries, I was definitely NOT in control. It was just an event that took place around me and that was the bit I did not like.

And this is what happened again tonight, and as I say, it all took place rather quickly too. But at least I knew that there was a beginning and an end in this case…well, sort of. It most certainly ended thank goodness. It was worrying though this time because of what actually happened. I had sensed fear and dread. Could I have died? Will I ALWAYS return from these jaunts?

I was tying myself up in knots thinking about it all. Tonight was serious. Perhaps I should speak with my father about it. He might open up again and tell me a bit more if he knows I'm worried.

And worried I was. It was the most anxious I'd ever felt regarding an 'experience'.

I spoke with him on the phone the next day and aired my feelings…and he DID divulge more. He drew a comparison between my motorbike and my mind.

"You've been working on your bike…you've added bits, you've adjusted bits…and you want to try it out and see what

36

it can do. Well, it's the same with your mind. There are probably bits being added...bits being adjusted..." ...he paused...

"Our future is not necessarily the sum of our past, Jamie...and it can all happen in a blink of an eye..."

Noncompliant Jock

I was now 24 and it was 1986.

I was still living in the capital, but I'd moved house and was renting a flat south of the river. My daytime courier work was still on the go, but it was part time now as I made more money by cash-in-hand taxi work at night.

I had started to get headaches. They had just begun out of the blue, and it was quite unusual for me as I never really suffered with that sort of thing. And unfortunately, it was not a headache that you just took a couple of Disprins for either. It was an excruciating head pain, and it would practically disable me when it occurred. I would have to stop whatever I was doing and try to control it, and this I found, after a while, that I actually could do. I also realised that the pain always seemed to start, and was worse, when I was in the presence of other people who were in close proximity. This was, of course, not good being a taxi driver, but after a while I'd worked out a solution. I would subtly distance myself from the person after a brief close encounter. It seemed to be that if someone came into my personal space of approximately two feet and stayed there for too long, I would be able to feel the onset of the headache. So, a simple turn of the head, or backing away, without appearing rude, would solve the problem and I could feel the pain almost immediately subsiding.

It sounded crazy, but it worked, and I felt in control of the situation again. However, I did think that if and when I get another girlfriend, the situation would be pretty awkward to say the least, so I made an appointment with my doctor.

It was around 9.30 a.m. and the waiting room was already full of coughs and colds.

"Come through!" he said, as his eyes connected with mine.

I got up and walked towards him as his hand instructed me to walk in front and down the corridor to his consulting room. I smiled as I knew the ways of this particular GP. He would use this technique to watch the patient walking. He reckoned he could tell a lot about a patient's well-being that way before they even got to his room.

I didn't do a silly walk, but I was tempted.

"Have a seat…Now, we haven't seen you for a while; so what brings you here today?"

I spoke of the headaches. I didn't go into too much detail about them other than I just took pain killers. But I did mention that they seemed to happen more when I was working and around people.

He asked a few questions about my occupation and busily scribbled upon a notepad. I could sense that he was going to go down the stress-at-work line.

"I need to examine you…take off your jacket…"

I stood up and removed it then sat back down as he slid over towards me on his stool.

"Lift up your shirt; I'm going to listen to your heart and lungs."

I obliged as he placed his stethoscope on my chest and then onto my back.

"He probably smokes…"

"Actually, I don't," I said.

I looked at his face. He was unblinkingly looking into my eyes; with an expression that I couldn't 'read' but at least he seemed vaguely interested. I don't mean to come across as being anti this doctor, far from it. I registered at this practice because of his excellent reputation as a GP when I first moved to London and I've stayed with the practice even though I've moved further away…not that I'm a regular visitor thank goodness.

It's just his manner. He comes over as aloof and superior. I'm sure he doesn't mean it. And it might be me being a bit picky, but that's the impression he gives.

He had slid back over to his desk now and was writing more notes. I was going to comment on the Ferrari on casters, but I kept quiet.

"Put your jacket back on."

It was spoken to the notepad rather than at me which made me purposefully stare at him as I stood up and tucked in my shirt. I can't help it, perhaps I AM being a bit picky, but there's no excuse for bad manners. "Manners maketh man" I would answer if anybody queried my exuberance in the attitude stakes, and this general lack of eye contact with almost 'instructive' comments annoyed me. I knew that he was like this though, and that his general bedside manner was always fairly command-like. It would never be a "Could you…" or an "if you wouldn't mind…"—it was just DO IT!

"Take a week off from work. I'm giving you a note. It will give you a chance to rest and clear your head. Keep on with the Disprin, and if the headaches don't go altogether, come back and see me."

I stood up, walked to the desk, and took the piece of paper. I then stretched out my other hand to which he reciprocated in a reactionary manner rather than a caring, routine, polite one, making eye contact with me for a millisecond then looking back down again at his notes.

"It's going to be a long day…"

I had slightly turned away, but looked back at the doctor who was still looking down.

"And for me as well," I said with a slight curtness.

He immediately looked up and I viewed a perturbed expression on his face as I turned towards the door.

"Wait!" he said suddenly, as he stood up.

"Wait a minute, please…can you…

…can you sit down again for a moment…?"

He was pointing at my empty chair with his hand. His manner had completely changed. There was true interest in his tone now as he constantly kept looking at me. I was puzzled.

I moved to the chair and sat back down.

"Do you know what I'm going to say?" he asked.

I felt rather awkward and I shifted slightly on the chair.

"I've absolutely NO idea what you're going to say," I replied with a slight nervous laugh in my voice.

He walked a couple of steps around towards me, stopped, and then slowly sat back on the edge of his desk.

"I think…you can read my thoughts…"

He said it slowly and deliberately, looking straight into my eyes.

"…and can you?" he inquisitively enquired, as he leaned slightly forward towards me with his head almost cocked to one side, his eyes unblinking and firmly focused on me.

Well…the feeling I had now resembled how I used to feel during school days when I was confronted with similar statements pertaining to my person, though the word 'confronted' is perhaps overdoing it somewhat as it never escalated into anything too awkward. It was never too serious, more like I had done something just a little bit naughty and had been found out, or a teacher had singled me out with a question thinking that I didn't know the answer because I wasn't listening, just to prove a point. Though, I always DID know, even if consciously I wasn't listening!

I had an idea that this might be a developing ability and that I could 'hear' people even though they were not speaking. I first noticed it when I was 'cabbing' a while back. It only happens now and then, and only it seems when I'm quite near the particular person which is what I was trying to avoid because of the headaches. It's difficult to know when it's actually taking place too as the voice I hear in my head IS their voice. It is like they are actually speaking normally to me, but without moving their lips…like a ventriloquist I suppose. I had given it some thought that it might be linked with the headaches too, but I was hoping that that might just be a coincidence.

So here I am, with the doctor putting me on the spot. And I responded how I always do in this sort of situation…

With slight embarrassment and then the need to…GET AWAY!

I left the GP's room, spurting out a load of apologetic garbled excuses to him. I was under pressure and my mouth was running on autopilot to fill the exit gap. Phweew, I was so relieved to be walking away outside and making tracks back home again.

That evening I sat and watched TV. I phoned the courier firm and told them that I'd been 'signed off' for a week, which they were surprisingly quite understandable about. I'd considered just dropping the courier job, and sticking with the evening taxi work which brought in much more money, anyway. Perhaps in a roundabout way this is what 'someone' was telling me to do.

I thought about it for a short while and then made a rather quick decision. Yes, I WOULD quit the courier day job and just concentrate on the taxi work. I could even expand that possibly into the daytime as well if I wanted too. It was down to me to get the work. If I didn't go out, I wouldn't get any money. It was as simple as that. I took advantage of the sick note, handed my notice in with the courier firm, with plans to return to taxiing on the following Saturday night.

I woke up on that Saturday morning rather early and I felt very different. My head was clear, unbelievably clear. It was like I'd been listening to a far off long wave radio station for ages and had suddenly re-tuned to an FM one.

And my body felt different. It was a strange feeling. I just knew that I was somehow physically stronger.

I looked at myself in the bathroom mirror, almost expecting to see another person looking back. I felt really peculiar, and I've got to be honest, and this may sound weird…but I felt powerful!

Something had happened. It was almost an overnight change. I'd gone to bed as Me 1 and had woken up as Me 2!

I looked at my hands and arms. It was a ridiculous feeling but they actually felt bigger. They were not bigger of course. They looked like my normal hands and arms, but my inner feeling was one of robustness and strength.

I looked back in the mirror again and moved my head from side to side as if checking my shaving technique. My neck felt tight and stiff.

I looked into the reflection of my own eyes and moved closer to the mirror…

I kept staring…

"John?" I said as I flinched back. Then I immediately realised what I had said…

"John? Who the bloody hell is John?" I said out loud rather strongly but I was laughing as I did. I then realised that I'd sworn. I never normally swear…well, I do but I'm aware of it when I do as it's not typical for me. My parents never really swear either, especially my mother. Once, when I was living with them, I was using an old hairdryer and the fuse blew. The dryer 'exploded' with such a loud bang that I reacted with, "BLOODY HELL!" I immediately turned and apologised to my mother who was sitting nearby, and she instantly forgave me because of the circumstances. I'm sure this all sounds quite over the top to someone who swears regularly, but that's the way we were, and are.

And just like back then, it came out, only this time it felt natural, and I also realised that I had suppressed the F word. I wanted to use it. I could hear the F word in my head…and I was going to say it…

"Who the FUCK is John?"

44

I stepped back from the mirror.

I felt REALLY, REALLY strange.

What is going on now?

I looked back at my reflection. It was me alright, but I felt so different and I certainly didn't feel the way that I looked…it was a weird feeling.

I walked into the kitchen and picked up the kettle. I looked at the handle, and as I held it, I began to squeeze it. I wanted to crush it! It was an instant thought and I applied more pressure and heard the plastic creaking. I COULD crush it if I wanted to, I know I could…but I stopped…and poured the 'old' water down the sink, refilled the kettle with fresh water, and plugged it in.

I felt so odd and SO really different.

It was now Saturday evening and I was preparing to get ready for my return to work. The car I drive is a dark blue Ford Cortina which I've had for approximately a year now. It's great for taxiing, quite economical, and so far has been quite reliable. I would always work around train stations in the city, mainly Charing Cross during the evenings, when bars would close and people would want to move on to the nightclub's.

It was close to 10 p.m. when I put on my leather jacket and made my way outside to the car. My frame of mind was strangely one of annoyance and I could not understand why.

I started the engine and immediately looked in the side pocket of the door…for my cigarettes! God, I needed one! The desire was there…and so were the cigarettes!

"I don't bloody smoke!" I said out loud as I placed one between my lips and fumbled for the lighter. I flipped the lid and thumbed the flint wheel in one very natural movement as the flame appeared, and then I leaned slightly forward and lit the cigarette. I breathed in the smoke and exhaled it upwards towards the roof almost immediately in a very routine like manner and drove off.

My body didn't feel like mine at all; that was probably the best way to describe it. It looked like mine but it just somehow didn't feel right. My thoughts were mixed too. I couldn't stop feeling grumpy and annoyed. I was never normally like that, never down in the mouth at all really. But tonight I felt irritated, I felt cross…but I couldn't understand why. The cigarette was so good though, and it was helping…I had been really bloody craving it, and I started to feel a little less anxious now that I had the thing between my lips.

I then suddenly thought of where I was going. Perhaps I was feeling cross because I was going to Charing CROSS? I smiled to myself at that ridiculous comparison. Good, I still had my silly sense of humour. I quickly looked in the rear view mirror and tried to see my reflection. I knew I was smiling…but…I couldn't see it!

I looked again.

I caught my dark image every now and then as the occasional street light mildly intensified the interior luminance, but I couldn't form a face, I couldn't make out MY face. I kept glancing in the mirror, leaning to the left, trying to see ME, but my actions were not acting in the reflection I was able to see…and I suddenly started to feel panicky. I saw glimpses of an outline of a face, and the more I tried to look the more perturbed I was becoming…

Then someone blasted their car horn and I reacted and pulled the steering wheel to the left…I had veered into the

46

centre of the road. I could feel exasperation building inside me as I gripped the wheel hard and looked for a place to pull over. I saw an entrance to a building where the road widened slightly and I pulled into the space and stopped.

I immediately grabbed the rear view mirror and angled it towards me. It was still too dark to make out anything. And frustratingly I knew there was no working interior light. "FOR FUCK'S SAKE!" I said out loud as I angrily pushed open the driver's door, threw my cigarette to the floor, and got out.

"Where've you been, Jock? Glasgow?" shouted the mocking man as he turned back to view the appreciating sniggers from his fellow compatriots. I glanced over at him, trying to think of something quick to say back…but it did not come. Instead, I shut the car door and made my way over to the makeshift table that was the command centre of the operation.

"Hey Jock; are you calling it a night?" came a voice. I could just make out a short woman leaning against the back wall smoking a rolled up cigarette. Her face was partially concealed in the shadows as she continued… "Because if you're not, I am!" She then came over, handed her spindly cigarette to me and walked off towards a group of parked cars.

I felt a bit confused. I didn't know any of these people. And the reference to the name Jock was wearing a bit thin. Frank called me that for fun because he knew I went up to Scotland a lot to visit my parents. But these people were all new drivers, I didn't know any of them, and where the fuck WAS Frank?

I took an annoying drag from the cigarette, and walked over to the back wall myself. I then glanced down at my watch, and moved my arm out quickly to catch a bit of light…

It was 4.05 a.m.

I suddenly focused, 4.05 a.m.! My mind was back.

What!…it can't be…it was only around 10 p.m. when I set out…and I've only just arrived here!

I froze, and it suddenly dawned on me that something was happening. Something that supposedly only happened to me was happening again, only this time I was living it. I wasn't recalling it and playing it back in my mind, it was happening NOW! And I was aware of it not being right and I was thinking about it…AS it was taking place!

I pulled up the collar on my jacket in reaction to a gust of wind, took another drag on the cigarette, and looked around.

The drivers were standing and talking in huddles. I moved slightly to one side to view their faces. I didn't recognise anyone! I took another drag on the cigarette as I heard the name 'Jock' mentioned again and I viewed a young lad who had come over to stand close by. He meant something to me for some reason but I couldn't understand why or how. I wanted to speak with him, and I did…but what I thought I said was not WHAT I said. I started to panic. My thoughts were not being acted on by my body! I walked over to my car and the lad followed.

My mind was racing. I couldn't relate my thoughts to any physical or verbal actions. I wanted to speak with this boy. I needed to, I wanted to, and I WAS, I was saying things…but he was not responding, and nor was my body.

I got into my car and the lad got in the back.

I started the engine and drove off. It was like I was in automatic mode. I was driving but I wasn't consciously thinking of driving. I could think but I couldn't put my thoughts into any communicative activity...though I knew that I was!

What was happening? It was like my whole being was being suppressed. My body was not responding to any of my thoughts.

The frustration in my mind was immense. I was trying to talk, and I WAS saying things. I could 'hear' myself, but it was obviously not audible or visible to this lad. And it was this lad that I wanted to talk with. I knew that I had to communicate with him. The desire to speak with him was so strong. But who was he? Why did I feel this way?

The car drove on.

I was now like a body within a body. In fact not even that. I was more like a mind within a mind that was within a body. And my mind had no influence over the other mind. I was just there...existing. But I could hear and I could see. I just could not affect anything. I was constantly 'saying' things but I guess it was all in my own mind. I could 'feel' my mouth forming the words, and I could 'hear' the sounds I was making, but there was nothing coming out in the real world...if this WAS the real world! My emotions were boiling over. I was in complete panic mode now as I focussed on what I was aware of, and that basically just came down to sight and sound.

I was so stressed, and I could feel the tension inside me...and then it happened!

My hand reached out and angled the rear view mirror...towards me.

I could see the face!

I could see the eyes and the nose; I could see them!

I wanted the head to lift up to see more, and it did, and I saw the mouth. This was not me! Oh my god…IT WAS NOT ME!

I was shouting, I was hollering, I was pointing and gesticulating…

But the hand just held the mirror as if content that it was showing me the face. This rugged, non-emotional, expressionless face, with eyes that looked straight into the depths of my soul.

It is its own being! It doesn't know I'm here! It cannot hear me or see me!

…And then the mirror was quickly readjusted to rear view and the hand placed back on the steering wheel.

Then the lad spoke!

And from being suddenly struck with horror at the face realisation and the instant heart pounding emotions that it instigated…I mentally refocused…on him!

I immediately calmed, and was listening and looking.

The car slowed down and came to a stop. I heard the boy's voice again, then the rear door opened…and then I heard it close.

I started to become 'vocal' once more. "Turn your head, TURN YOUR HEAD!" but my only view was of the road in front…

Then the car started to move…

I kept 'shouting' as it slowly went down the road; I was 'turning my head' but my view was only forwards, as we rounded a corner and then accelerated away.

I knew that the lad had got out and was now a distance behind…

I was still and quiet. My purpose had gone, whatever that purpose was, because I felt empty, I really did. The determination and resolve I had was no more and I could feel my mind wandering…I wasn't seeing the road, I wasn't focusing on anything. I was travelling aimlessly with no defining thoughts to direct me; it was like a dream presentation. There were images and feelings of movement triggering the minutest memory stimulations, but I could not understand why…and then suddenly all I was aware of was…

Blackness.

A dark space of nothingness, it was just there in front of me!

I 'stared' straight ahead and waited…

I knew that it wasn't flat…it had depth, it had width, it was open and vast. I couldn't 'see' that it did, I just knew. Then the black became blacker, it became a rich, deep, intense black and I was aware of the occasional almost insignificant pinprick flashes of white light. One to the right, then one lower down to the left, then up to the top right, gradually increasing in numbers like tiny stars, over and over and over…and then…it stopped.

I felt completely at ease, so calm, and so serene as I continued to 'stare,' still waiting, anticipating something. I should know what is going to happen, shouldn't I? I've done this before, haven't I?

'BEEP BEEP BEEEEeeeeeeeeeeeep!'

I was standing in the road as a car drove by with its horn blaring!

I reacted immediately, throwing a hand in the air at the undeserving noise.

I stood still for a few seconds, irritatingly watching the fading red lights blend into the distance, as the purring sound of my car engine suddenly aurally refocused me. I turned round, got back in and pulled the door shut.

Then…as if a switch had been thrown, my mind was awash with what had happened and I grabbed the rear view mirror and swivelled it towards me. I still couldn't see properly in the gloom but as I felt my face with my hand I caught a slight image of the contours to convince myself that it was MY face! I then swivelled my neck and looked out of the side window and then back to look at the car dashboard lights in one conscious movement…and yes, thankfully I was in control of my actions too!

I sat there staring out of the car as I gradually tried to come to grips with what had just happened. The relief that the experience was over was immense. I'd not felt panic, in the true sense of the word, like that before. I'd been trapped inside the mind and body of this man called Jock…yes, Jock! I almost pulled back in the driver's seat when the name registered again. These people knew him. He WAS someone. Jock was not just a name that I was jokingly referred to by Frank, but actually a living person.

It was all too much to take in, and the need to get back home suddenly became a priority.

With that thought, I instinctively pulled back my jacket sleeve and manoeuvred my wrist so that there was a bit of light from the street falling onto my watch.

It was 10.10 p.m.…

…I did a double take…10.10 p.m.?

WHAT?

I froze again as I tried to digest the fact that only about 10 minutes had passed since I'd left home!

Oh, my goodness!

I leant forward and turned the ignition key, and there followed a horrible grinding sound as the starter motor tried to turn over an engine that was already running.

"Argghhh!" I reacted out loud, as I put the car in gear, did a U-turn, and drove straight back home.

Distant Parents

It was Sunday.

I awoke and started gathering my thoughts about last night as I lay there staring at the ceiling.

Things were getting much more serious now. The events of this other time and place were now merging into real time it seemed. That is, if this real time IS the real time. Who knows? This other time and place could be the real time and I could be in dreamland myself now for all I knew.

And who was this boy, this lad? And why did I feel so strongly about communicating with him?

I tried to remember his face, but I couldn't picture him. I wasn't even sure if I actually looked at him properly. But the lad's voice seemed to trigger something inside me. And the more I thought about it, the more I felt close to him. I smiled to myself as I questioned my sexual orientation for a moment...just for a moment. No, I definitely wasn't homosexual. And anyway, the feelings that I had were more of preservation and protection towards this boy. It was almost a feeling of admiration, like I wanted to put him on a pedestal for some reason. And that was so puzzling; I had no reason to think like that. I hadn't met this lad before, I knew nothing about him…and yet, something inside me said the complete opposite.

I got out of bed and went and made myself some cereal for breakfast.

My mind started to surge again with the feelings from last night as I stood there eating. The anxiety and sheer panic was so scary when I realised that my actual existence had suddenly been compressed within the shell of this other body. Like I said earlier, I had felt trapped. My mind was active but I could not communicate or activate any physical movement myself. The trouble was, I felt like I WAS communicating. I could hear myself talking and shouting, and I could feel the physical movement. My brain was telling me that I was doing the things I was trying to do, but I could see that it was NOT actually taking place. The expression 'it's all in the mind' rang true, because in the mind was where it was ONLY happening.

'Ding dong ding dong'…my track of thought was interrupted by the musical sounds of my front doorbell. I glanced at my watch. It had just gone 8.00 a.m. I put the cereal bowl down on the kitchen top and walked towards the door.

"Who the heck's this at this time?" I said out loud.

I kicked my plimsolls, which were lying in the hallway, to one side, as I unlocked the door and pulled it open.

A tall, rather smart looking man was standing there dressed in a leather jacket and dark trousers.

He looked vaguely familiar as he began to speak…

"He knew you'd done it anyway…"

"I'm sorry?" I responded, completely perplexed.

The man turned and started to walk away.

I moved forward and leant out of the door…

"Excuse me, excuse me…what are you going on about, who are you?"

I was raising my voice but was quite calm. I was just taken aback by the oddness.

The man stopped and looked back.

We made eye contact and then there was almost a pause in time as we looked at each other. I knew I wanted to say something but I didn't know what. I could feel my mind trying to create words but I couldn't speak them…and then he turned, raised an arm briefly, and continued walking away.

I knew this chap, didn't I? I couldn't place him though, but I was sure that I recognised him from somewhere. I hesitated for a moment, and then sprang into action. I quickly looked down to the floor looking for my plimsolls and pulled them on, almost falling over as I did, and then practically fell out of the door.

I looked up the road. Where did he go, he'd gone! He couldn't possibly have got up to the crossroads that quickly. I turned around and looked in the opposite direction. There was no one to be seen!

I looked back up towards the crossroads again. Even if the chap had run, I would have surely seen him before he turned the corner.

"You alright mate?"

It was a voice from above. I looked up. It was one of my neighbours leaning out of his window.

The question was one of concern, but probably mixed with one of annoyance too at the noise on an early Sunday morning.

"Yeah, sorry," I replied, as I looked back down the road again. I paused. I was rather confused... "...err yeah sorry," I added again. "I'm fine, thanks."

I gave a reassuring and apologetic gesture up to my neighbour, then turned and headed back inside. I wanted to go up to the crossroads, but the 'conversation' had made me feel like I should retreat out of sight for a bit.

I shut the door and as I turned to walk into the kitchen, I glanced at my reflection in the full length hall mirror. Yes, I recognised that face...it was still me. I semi-smiled to myself at my need to check...and then suddenly it struck me! I knew who that man was at the door!

It was Danny!

It was Dave's biker friend, Danny! Well, it certainly looked like Danny...it was those eyes...I'm sure it was him!

I put down the cereal bowl that I'd just picked up and stared blankly.

I hadn't spoken with Dave since I'd moved house. In fact, I hadn't seen Dave since the ride-out on the bikes that night, which must be a good two years ago. I'd delivered a parcel now and then to his house, but Dave had never been in. Our friendship just seemed to peter-out...though I know I didn't do much to prevent it.

But the more I thought about it; I convinced myself that it must have been Dan. But how? And why? Dave didn't know where I had moved to, let alone Danny. It was ridiculous to think that it was him, but his face and in particular his eyes resembled the image I had of him in my mind.

I sat down, then immediately got back up and looked for my address and telephone book. I started flicking through the pages...Yes! There it was, Dave's telephone number.

I waited until lunch time and then dialled the number. No reply.

I tried a few more times in the afternoon, but again no reply.

I'd decided to delay taxiing until tomorrow now, so I tried phoning again later that evening.

Dave answered.

Apologies and excuses were at the forefront of my conversation at first and I started to feel quite guilty for not attempting to keep in contact. It works both ways, but it was me who had moved away without saying anything, and it was that that Dave kept referring to, albeit in a jokey type manner really. But I could sense the underlying feeling…

"Have you heard much from Danny?"

Dave paused, and then replied, "No…well, he's still missing."

I queried what Dave meant and he explained that he didn't find out for a few days afterwards when the police called, but Danny had not returned home that night of the bike ride, and now over two years had gone by, and he's still classed as 'missing'.

"Oh my god!" I exclaimed as my mind recoiled at the information. "I know, it's not good," continued Dave. "He'd done things similar to this before where he would suddenly not turn up at the pub and disappear off the radar. But it would only be for about a week at the most."

"Where does he go then? I asked."

"He goes down the coast apparently…that's what he said anyway…but for this long?"

I was stunned, and I didn't know what to say. Well, I did…but I couldn't…not now. How could I say that Danny had turned up on my door-step? No, it just didn't make sense and it didn't seem right to mention it. Especially as I didn't know for 100 percent that it WAS him anyway? It would give false hopes to all concerned…no, it would be awful.

"Do you know where on the coast he goes?" I enquired.

"Dan keeps himself to himself. I don't even know where he lives let alone where he would've gone," replied Dave with a laugh.

I asked some more about Danny but Dave didn't enlighten me on anything new and after a bit of conversation on our bikes we wished each other well and said our goodbyes. There were promises of get-togethers in the near future, but I knew that it probably wouldn't materialise.

I put the phone back on its holder and turned to walk away.

It immediately started ringing.

"Helloooo…"

"Hi, it's mum!"

"Oh hello mum, I'm so glad you said it was you, I never would have…"

"Stop it Jamie, listen…" she interrupted… "Your father has had to go to hospital. Bit of a long story, but I'm just about to get a taxi over to see him now."

Her shortened story was that he had been admitted into hospital last night after a fall. He'd knocked himself out but had regained consciousness and seemed to be improving. She hadn't phoned any earlier because he was on the mend, and she didn't think it serious enough to bother me. But now the hospital had just phoned saying that he'd lost consciousness again.

I glanced at the wall clock. It was just before 7.30 p.m. I'd be up there in the early hours sometime if I left now.

"Do not even THINK about driving up tonight, I'm getting a taxi over to see him in a few minutes. I just wanted to let you know. I'll phone you later when I get back; tell you how he is."

I had already decided.

"Mum...I'm leaving as soon as I can. I'll go straight to the hospital. I'll see you there or back at the house."

I knew exactly where the hospital was too. I'd been there with him before when he'd hurt his back a few years ago.

I quickly put a few essentials in a holdall and after a quick check around the flat I walked to the door. I put the bag down and looked at my watch; imaginarily drawing the hour hand around 6 times on the watch face. "Going to be there around 1.30'ish then with a bit of luck," I said out loud.

It was a good journey up. Traffic was quite light and almost non-existent when I got over the border and onto the A74.

There was a lot of thinking time too. I was concerned about my father but I kept thinking about the 'visit' by Danny, and I was fairly convinced that it WAS Danny too. I was so annoyed that I'd lost sight of him outside the flat. If only I hadn't bothered about putting on those wretched plimsolls it would have been a different story. But WHERE did he go? And what did he mean by what he said?

I parked the car in a rather empty hospital car park and walked over to the front entrance and went inside. A nurse at the desk looked up, and I asked after my father. She expressed her amazement that I had just driven up from London as we walked along the corridor; then she directed me into a ward.

"He's just down the end there on the right," she said almost whispering.

"Yeah, I can hear him," I retorted quietly with a laugh in my voice.

"He's still unconscious I'm afraid," said the nurse as she looked at me quizzically… "But there's your mother with him, if you want to go through," she continued as she pointed. "…I'll leave you all be."

I looked towards the nurse wanting to query what she'd said about my father, but she had already turned and was walking away.

My mother looked very tired as she greeted me with a hug and thanked me for coming up, and then she sat back down and took hold of my father's hand as she whispered, "Look who's here, Arthur…"

I switched my attention towards him.

"Is he still unconscious, mum?" I questioned, rather louder than I wanted.

"Yesssss he is…and shhhhhh, everyone's asleep," said my mother as she gestured to the other beds.

That was weird; I knew that I had heard him. I had heard his voice. I wasn't clear what he said, but I was sure that it WAS his voice.

I hesitated as I glanced at my mother.

"Look at him," she said as she reverted her focus back to him… "It's like he's just sleeping."

I pulled up a chair and sat down next to her.

"And you need some sleep as well mum…come on, why don't we make a move back, and we can come up and visit tomorrow morning."

She hesitated…and then slowly nodded her head in agreement. She then looked at my father and lent forward and gave him a kiss on the cheek. "We're going to make a move now, Arthur," she said quietly… "We'll be back to see you in the morning."

I looked at my father as she stood up and pulled the chair back against the wall. I moved forward. I felt I should give my father a kiss too. It was something I'd never done before as an adult, but there was something there telling me that I should. I leant over and kissed him on the forehead.

"Thanks for coming up boy, look after your mother."

I reeled back.

"What's wrong," said Jane as she grabbed my arm.

"It's dad! He just spoke to me! He just thanked me for…" Then I stopped as I looked back at my father, almost realising immediately that he hadn't spoken a word.

My mother still had a hand on my arm and as I looked at her I could see her eyes beginning to well-up.

"Oh goodness…I'm sorry; I wish this could've been different."

She turned away from me for a few moments, and then she turned back.

"Mum? What do you mean?" I could see that she was getting rather emotional.

She paused before her reply… "…I'm sorry…your father always believed that it was best that you found out in your own way how you would develop…and in your own time…and look what's happened now!"

She looked back at my father.

"You should have spoken with him properly…I told you this would happen," she said in slightly raised reprimanding tones as she leaned towards him. Then she took a handkerchief out of her bag and wiped her eyes…

I noticed a nurse walking over…

"I'm sorry, would you mind if you both could leave soon," she said.

I understood her saying that. I felt a bit awkward because of the time, and that we were the only visitors there, AND because of the 'hushed' noise we were making!

"No that's fine, I'm really grateful that you allowed me to stay…thank you…we're going right now," responded my mother as she composed herself and gave me a look that said, "Let's go!"

We both walked down the ward and out of the hospital front entrance and over to my car.

As I closed the door, I turned to her and said, "I heard him mum…as clear as day."

She turned and looked at me in the dimly lit lights of the car park, "Yes…I know…I know you heard him."

I looked at my mother. She said it in a weary, almost resigned manner, but also with a somewhat authoritative outward bearing.

"Come on, let's go home. Let's get some sleep, and we'll talk about it in the morning," she added as she yawned.

As I drove back I was thinking about my mother's attitude. It had changed. Although she was weepy in the hospital, she appeared quite assertive, which was very unlike her. I even noticed it earlier on the phone when she told me of my father's predicament.

We spoke only briefly on the journey back, probably due to tiredness more than anything, but I couldn't stop thinking that my father had spoken to me, and that I had 'heard' him…in my mind, and that hopefully he would be OK.

The next morning I awoke to the smell of bacon cooking as my mother prepared another fried breakfast. Nothing had changed there.

I got dressed and went into the kitchen.

"Morning! Good timing," she said, "did you sleep alright?"

We spoke for a while about my taxi work and life generally in London, whilst she scurried around. It was just the same; tea cloth in hand, wiping surfaces, adjusting this, moving that. She just liked to be always doing something all the time.

As soon as I'd put my knife and fork down, she was there whisking my plate off to the sink. I laughed, "Hold on! I was just having a rest!"

She paused and looked at me, "I'm joking, I'm joking…" I said.

She continued washing up the plate, then, as she put it on the draining board, she wiped her hands with a towel and came over and sat opposite me at the table.

I smiled. This was like old times. My parents would always use this tactic if they wanted to say something important or serious to me, and it looked like my mother was going to keep with tradition.

"This is tricky," she said as she slowly exhaled.

Her line of focus had moved away from my eyes, and she looked over my shoulder at the wall behind, almost seemingly searching for a satisfactory way to begin.

I looked at her. My mother normally had an air of ease about her. She always portrayed a non-opinionated, just getting on with life type attitude, who would agree with my father in most cases to probably just ensure an uncomplicated existence. But her expressions and witty verbal responses to different situations that I had witnessed over the years, told me that she was a much deeper woman than she showed. And I could sense this now and even last night. I'd never seen her on her own like this since probably my school days, when my father was at work. She was 'in-charge,' almost fending for her-self so to speak, and the air about her now…was different.

"I need to tell you some things…" she continued, and then she paused.

"…and I just want you to listen to me…don't ask me anything until I've finished, OK?"

I started to feel concerned, "Is dad going to be alright?"

"It's not about your father, well, it is and it isn't…it's about YOU…and I said, DON'T ask me anything until I'd finished!"

She smiled as she raised her voice with the last few words, and I smiled back.

"I'm not going to say that I know it all, because I don't. I know very little, and I know that you know that we know that you know…" …and then she laughed.

I looked at her with an exaggerated bewildered expression, but I knew that she knew that I knew that they knew…(*sorry*).

"What you said last night…that you could hear your father…well, it tells me that your mental abilities are developing further…and it scares me…well actually, it scares me a lot. It's not knowing why…why you have these gifts and what is the reason? Your father knows much more than he wants me to know and I'm sure he's protected us from something over the years…but I'm just not sure what?"

"Can I speak now?" I said slightly sarcastically.

She smiled…

"Well, you've got ME scared now."

"Oh I'm sorry Jamie; I didn't mean it to come over like that…no, don't be worried," she continued, "It's just me thinking. I've been kept in the dark about this since you were a baby. Your father always said that he wanted you to discover who you really are in your own way. Sorry, I didn't mean it like that, I mean…to discover your talents, and just let them develop naturally without you having information that would allow you to pre-empt what might happen."

She paused…

"…Oh, I don't know…perhaps it was wrong to do it like that."

She paused again and looked at me. I was about to speak, but she spoke again.

"Can you control it now? Can you visit when you want to?"

I looked at her. I knew what she meant of course, but it was so strange hearing it being asked, and also in the way that she was asking it. It was like she'd known all along that it was going to happen; it was just a case of when!

I felt myself getting slightly annoyed…

"I think you are assuming things, mum. You're assuming things that I should know that I don't know."

"Oh…I'm sorry, I'm really sorry. Let's stop, because I'm saying things out of turn and you're getting cross. This isn't right; we should've had this conversation years ago."

She got up and came around the other side of the table. "Come here," she said as she beckoned me to stand up and then she gave me a hug. I could sense her sadness and exasperation as we cuddled. "It's OK mum, it's OK…we just need to get dad better and then we can all sit down and have a talk."

"And I hope he does get better too."

"He will, of course he will," I said reassuringly.

My mother pushed back with her hands on my shoulders and paused…

"You heard MY thoughts didn't you?"

I looked into her eyes. This was like the doctor's surgery all over again.

"I didn't say anything," she continued, "I was just thinking about your father's health. It was like last night with Dad, you heard him too…can you control it now? Can you listen when you want too?"

I felt myself getting slightly agitated again because of all this sudden questioning and this true realisation of ME. I'd been different like this since around 8 years old, although it had taken years for things to truly develop, but develop it has, and now I was feeling slightly overwhelmed with it all; I think that was the best way to describe it. My mother was placing me right in her spotlight and that was particularly odd too because she'd never done that before. And the whole of this now makes me think about my past life living and growing up with my parents.

Was it all a sham or am I just getting carried away with it all? I shouldn't think this way I know, as they have given me loads of support over the years, and I've never wanted for anything…except perhaps, answers. And I've sort of understood their reasoning, or should I say my father's reasoning, for not wanting to divulge too much. But I think now I really want to know!

"No, I can't…it just seems to happen…and more so when I'm close to the person as well, though I'm sure I heard dad last night when I first came into the ward."

"…well, that certainly wasn't close, was it? Have you been able to listen for long? Though I get the impression it's all fairly new?"

"No, not long, and I think this new ability was linked with bad headaches that I was getting too, but thankfully they've subsided now" I replied… "And to be honest, I've only just realised that I was doing it…but…I reckon I might have been able to for a while now…and anyway, I definitely 'heard' dad! He must have known I could 'hear' as well because he actually spoke to me!"

Jane paused and gradually started to smile, "I think he was probably trying you out."

Her face reflected her thoughts of my father and I smiled too.

"Has he got this gift too then?"

She hesitated… "No, no…he hasn't. It's just you."

"But why, I mean…why JUST me…and how did I come by it? Are there others, do you know of other people like me too?"

My emotions were changing like the wind, and I started to get slightly frustrated again by it all.

My mother had moved away from me and walked over to the kitchen top and turned around.

"We don't, well...I don't know. I'm sorry. I don't mean to be cagey about it all. He told me very little over the years, so I simply do not know enough to explain it all."

I looked down at the kitchen table. My mind was whirring around and I was getting frustrated. Then I looked back up...

"I don't get it. If he knows, how does he know? And why didn't he ever want YOU to know? You're my mother and father, so how come he knows more about me than you do! It's crazy, and why didn't you ask him mum, why didn't you ask him more?"

Jane took a big intake of breath... "Look...like you said, let's get dad better and then we can sit down and have a good old talk."

I looked back down at the kitchen table again and reflected on my mother's words.

"I know, I know..."

I calmed down and apologised for getting angry. I knew it was not my mother's fault that she didn't know, but what I couldn't understand was why she really hadn't asked more questions over the years.

But then, that's the relationship my mother and father had. She always believed everything he said. She never queried anything, so I suppose there was never any uncertainty or doubt in her mind. It was just the way they were. Or more like, just the way they had been, because I was now seeing my mother in a new light, a much stronger and assertive light. I didn't know why the change, but it was clear to me that she was different.

Visiting times were from 2 p.m. to 5 p.m. and my mother had made a point of saying that we should not abuse that because of how accommodating the nurses had been last night. I agreed, and we arrived just after the hour and made our way to the ward.

My father was still unconscious.

"Has there been any improvement?" asked Jane as she looked at Arthur and then at the nurse.

"No, I'm sorry, there's been no change...but he's comfortable."

"What's happening then, do you think? Why is he still unconscious?" I said, as the nurse turned to look at him.

"Well, we're waiting for various test results at the moment; otherwise we're not sure I'm afraid. The doctors say that the bump on the head has affected something because other than that, he seems OK. It's like he's having a long sleep."

"I said that last night," responded Jane as she looked back at Arthur. "Come on, I know you like a long lay in, but this is ridiculous."

The nurse smiled, and so did I. But this talk from my mother was again so different from her normal ways. So much so that I felt myself staring in bewilderment at her in an almost vain attempt to receive reasons for it all.

"Would you like some tea or coffee?"

The nurse's question broke off my gaze and we both accepted the rather nice offer of two teas as she walked away.

"Can you hear your father now?" said Jane rather quickly as soon as the nurse was out of earshot.

I looked towards him. "No...there's nothing..." I paused as I kept looking. "No, I can hear nothing, nothing at all."

"Move closer, go right up to him," said my mother rather eagerly.

I moved towards the bed, noting my mother's assertive tone again.

I hovered over my father almost like I was going to kiss him once more, looking into his closed eyes.

"No mum, there's nothing. To be honest, I don't know how I'm supposed to hear."

"You don't have to do anything," retorted Jane, "It's automatic."

I stood back and looked at her.

"And how do you know that?"

"Because I do…" she replied quickly again, as she turned her attention back to Arthur.

"Good afternoon, good afternoon, I'm Dr Taylor."

Jane looked back at the tall, grey haired, bespectacled man, in a white coat, standing at the bottom of the bed.

"Good afternoon," she said, turning to face him, as I stretched out my hand automatically to greet him.

"The brain stem was damaged when he had the fall…and unfortunately, this is why he is not regaining consciousness."

Straight to the point I thought!

I could tell my mother was taken aback by the suddenness of his remarks as she looked back at my father and then at the doctor. "So, what does that mean? Long term I mean? Is he going to get better?"

The doctor paused…

"He's in a coma, and it does seem to have gone a little deeper as compared to yesterday…" He paused again. "Let's wait and see…"

My mother was still looking back at Arthur and holding his hand. I didn't know what to say. This was now serious stuff. I suddenly realised that I actually may not have my father back.

"Two teas, and there's some sugar in the bowl if you need some." The nurse had returned, putting the drinks on the bedside cabinet, and reacted as she became aware of our probable ashen looking faces.

The doctor used the convenient opportunity to leave.

"Oh dear," she said. "Isn't it good news?"

Jane gave a long exhale of breath, "it doesn't seem like it…what was the name of that doctor again?"

I think the nurse could probably tell by my mother's expression and tone that she didn't want to send him a Christmas card.

"It was Dr Taylor. I'm sorry…he can be a bit blunt sometimes. He doesn't mean…"

"No, don't worry," Jane interrupted. "It's OK…it's not going to change anything."

I nodded my head slowly in agreement at my mother's backtracking…

"I'll leave you both with your teas," said the nurse as she started to retreat.

It was my turn now to let out a long exhale of breath.

My mother turned to me, "Try listening again! Go up close…see if you can hear him."

There was an agitated panic in her voice now as I immediately responded and went around the other side of the bed, put a hand on my father's shoulder, and leaned towards him.

I could 'hear' nothing and I felt odd. I really didn't know what I was doing and how I should be doing it. Should it just happen like she said, or should I be 'listening' in a certain way?

I felt frustrated as I looked at my father laying there. I was willing him to say something, to be able to hear anything from him.

I shook my head slowly from side to side. "There's nothing mum. I can't hear…"

"Just focus on him!" she interrupted. "Relax and focus. Just imagine dad saying something to you. Listen with your mind. Focus and listen."

This was so difficult. I wanted to hear. I wanted to hear my father so much. And I knew my mother was now desperate for me to hear too.

I looked back at my father and then closed my eyes. I squeezed his shoulder, "Come on dad, say something to me; say anything…"

"Just listen…listen!" insisted Jane again, "open your mind…" she paused as she looked back at Arthur. "It's automatic…if he's there, you'll hear him…"

I felt panicky now. Is she saying that if I don't hear him, he's NOT there?

I looked over to the nurses at their desk. They were smiling at something they were reading. I felt conspicuous. It was like I was doing something I should not be doing. I closed my eyes again and 'focused' on my father. "Come on Dad, please…please…please" I said in my mind…willing my father to respond.

And then suddenly…he spoke, and he laughed as he did. My persistence had worn him down.

"Alright, alright, but just go careful then…and I want it back in one piece," he said in a defeated tone.

I opened my eyes…

I could see the speeding bikes up ahead and I was catching them. The rear rider was my target. I had to get to him. It was imperative.

For a moment I questioned the reason, but almost immediately the thought was gone. It was logged in my mind that the rider had to be stopped, that was all that mattered, and I needed to get to him and stop him…NOW!

The night time air rushed past at pace as my car moved nearer and nearer. A left-handed 90 degree sloping bend next, followed by a straight piece of road. That's when I would catch up with him. I knew the route and I knew that's when it would happen. My car edged out onto the other side of the road, as the rear bike took the bend ahead.

I tried to correct the line and steer back but my car continued on the opposite side, accelerating faster and faster into the corner.

I shouted and screamed at the thought of a head on collision. Nooooooo! The adrenalin was pumping; my heart was pounding, as sheer panic took over my mind. I wasn't doing this! I wasn't driving! I was holding the steering wheel and I was turning it, but it wasn't responding…I was NOT in control!

The car took the bend on the wrong side of the road as if it was on rails, and then accelerated out of it onto the straight that lay ahead, crossing back over to the correct side.

"MY GODDDDDD!" I shouted out in total relief that nothing had been coming the other way, and then the rush of exhilaration filled my head, as the realisation of what had just happened immediately kicked in… "WHOOOOOOOOOOOOOOO!"

I gripped the steering wheel tight and was aware that my right foot was pushed hard against the floor as I raced up the road behind the bike. My mind had refocused…It's got to happen now! It has to take place in the next few seconds! Anything else didn't matter! I quickly manoeuvred alongside the speeding bike. I was back in control. I glanced across to see the open face helmet rider looking back. His expression, seen for a fraction of a second, was one of surprise and unease as my outstretched arm and hand swiftly eclipsed his face in an instant. I was beckoning the rider to stop! Telling him to stop! DEMANDING him to stop…as I drove onto my parents driveway, turned off the lights and then the engine. I sat there thinking for a moment. How was I going to get away with this? Those damned bollards, I just didn't see them!

I leaned forward and looked up at the windows of the house. No lights were on, everyone was in bed.

I got out of the car and went around the back to inspect the damage again. The driver's side rear light was broken and the bumper slightly bent inwards. My father's words, "and I want it back in one piece," suddenly 'played' in my mind. Well, it was still sort of in one piece. It just needed some of the pieces adjusting.

The next morning I left early for work on my motor-scooter. My father was still asleep but I'd spoken briefly with my mother who had got up to see me off. I didn't mention the car's situation. I should have done as I felt quite guilty on the ride into work. I had the respite of the morning, but it was just delaying the inevitable. Hopefully he would have calmed down by the time I got back. That's what I was hoping anyway.

I finished my Saturday morning shift at 12.30 p.m. as normal and was soon riding back home. I had no option, I just had to come clean and say to him what had happened. I reversed into a bollard. It was as simple as that. I'll never be allowed to borrow his prized possession again, that's for sure. He had always said "No," but I had pestered him and badgered him and my perseverance had worn him down, and I was thinking all of this as I parked my Lambretta down the side of the house. I opened the back door and walked into the kitchen. My mother was preparing lunch, "Hello love…you'd better not talk to your dad at the moment; he's in a foul mood…"

I opened my mouth to respond but she continued, "…someone drove into the car in the car park this morning."

"What!" I responded rather quickly, "oh no!"

Thankfully, I could always put on the right face for the right situation.

My thoughts were of total relief; my expression was of total concern!

"Yes, we came back with our shopping and dad noticed that the back light was broken and the bumper was bent. He said that it's typical of the people of today…they're so dishonest. There was no note left or anything!"

I slowly shook my head from side to side in an excellent portrayal of disbelief and sympathy with my mother's words.

I'd gone too far with my mannerisms, conduct and expressions. I couldn't back track and admit it now could I?—though the words, "they're so dishonest," did hit home…

…I closed my eyes and just sent my thoughts… "*It was me, Dad. I did it.*"

I opened my eyes and squeezed my father's shoulder again and then looked across the bed at my mother's face.

She seemed much calmer and less anxious as she focused on my eyes…

"You didn't hear him," she said, "…but I'm sure he heard you."

We left the hospital just before 5 p.m. and made our way back to the house.

I was feeling quite strange. What happened to me earlier was very different. It wasn't just one other time and place, It was two, and they merged seamlessly together. The scary bit was that it had all taken place in a second or two…perhaps not even that…just in a blink of an eye! And when I say 'all taken place', I mean hours and hours!

In the jaunt at my parents' old place I actually went to bed there, slept, and then woke up and went to work for the morning…and only a SECOND had passed in real time! The more I think about it, the more incredible it seems. There are too many questions now that I can ask. Questions that would have me pulling my hair out trying to get ANYWHERE near an answer.

My mother was filling up the kettle as she looked over at me.

For a second it was déjà vu as I sat down at the kitchen table.

"Come on love, talk to me. Tell me everything!" she said, as she took two mugs out of the cupboard.

"I know something happened to you at the hospital…so tell me."

I decided to stay over at the house that night, and we spent most of it talking about my 'jaunts.' She was calm and understanding and not once did she express amazement or astonishment. Her responses were more of empathy and she assured me that I would be able to influence and control them once I learned how too.

"How can you be so sure?…you don't know that…and how do I learn anyway?" was my immediate frustrated reaction.

She looked at me.

It was a look that didn't seem right coming from her. It was difficult to explain that properly…

"Dad said to me once…that the day will come when you will know everything that there is to know about everything…so…just wait Jamie…just wait…"

I smiled, but I don't know why. It was probably in accepting defeat in my questioning if anything.

She then went on to say how proud she was of me and how I had not let it all 'go to my head' over the years. Especially she said, around the time when I'd left home, because neither she nor my father were around to keep the inquisitive prying types at bay.

To be honest, it was fine. I think I managed it easier then anyway, because I was starting out 'on my own' and it was all new to me, and there was not an already established prying set of people to be aware of.

She also said again that she was concerned about NOT knowing where the journey was going to take me.

I know she meant the journey of my life, but I was also wondering where the NEXT 'jaunt journey' would take me!

We reiterated again before we retired for the night that we'd get dad back on his feet first, and then we'd all have this long overdue chat and get everything out in the open…

…We lost the chance…

The phone rang early around 7 a.m. the next day and I heard my mother gasp when the hospital broke the terrible news that my father had passed away during the night.

She was inconsolable, and I did my best to comfort her and I was glad that I was there to do so.

I tried to stay strong and supported her over the coming days, and ensured that the relevant requirements that needed to take place were put into motion. It was a horrible time, and my mother was understandably heartbroken, but I never cried. My only emotion was anger, and it was directed towards life. How can it be so lovely one minute and then so awful the next? I kept thinking about my father, and the more I thought, the more I got exasperated. I loved my father, but there was always something about him that I never fully understood. I couldn't explain it. It was just a feeling that had built over the years. But now that he had gone it was playing on my mind more than ever.

I always thought that he was more complex than he portrayed. That he may have had many thoughts, beliefs and ideas that he never shared. But the strongest feeling was that he was deliberately withholding something that affected me and probably my mother too.

I'd always felt that, and after my recent talk with her, that feeling had been confirmed. But during my life I'd always dismissed it. If my father had something to say to me, and it was important, I felt that he would've said. Though deep down, I always thought that the day would come when he would say..."Boy, I need to tell you some things." That was always there in the back of my mind. There was this unspoken 'understanding' that I had with my father. An understanding that was probably a little more biased on his side than mine.

In hindsight I should've really questioned him. I should've queried things, asked more, and not taken his 'finishing routine' to conversations AS the finish…but unfortunately I had done what my mother had done…

And now…it was all too late.

I stayed in Scotland until a few days after the funeral, which was organised very calmly and considerately by a local village undertaker. It was a quiet gathering of just friends and neighbours as we had no other family, and afterwards there was a reception arranged at a nearby hotel. Everyone from the funeral gathering was invited, although it was noted that a man and a woman of foreign descent, who were present at the funeral, did not attend. I asked my mother who they were but she did not know. She said they acknowledged her by nodding/bowing their heads but that they'd disappeared before she could speak with them. It was assumed that they were friends of neighbours who wanted to pay their respects, but it transpired that all the neighbours did not know them either. And as in typical British fashion, everyone just went along with the proceedings and no one said anything at the time. My mother's immediate neighbours Celia and Tom said that the 'two foreigners', as they were called, seemed like they wanted to stay out of everybody's way. I sort of understood what they meant by that. I did 'catch' the ladies' eye quite a few times though and we exchanged smiles, but as they didn't come to the hotel gathering, and all the flowers and cards seemed to be accounted for, who they were remained a mystery.

The next three months were quite demanding and punishing.

I tried to visit my mother near enough every weekend to make sure that she was coping. And each time I saw her I noticed that her behaviour was always different. She was understandably withdrawn at first, but then on subsequent visits it became obvious to me that her character was changing. Her body language and demeanour always came across as never the same as the time before, and I could see that her reasoning and understanding skills had deteriorated. It was odd.

I contacted her doctor and arranged a home visit as I knew my mother had also become concerned about leaving the house for any given length of time too. I raised my concerns with the G.P mentioning how rapidly I thought she was changing, and unfortunately for the worse.

After examining her, the doctor said that the loss of my father had most definitely caused her deterioration, but also added that her mental change had been quite dramatic since he'd seen her at her last check-up, and he told me that he had organised various tests to be carried out to ascertain whether 'anything else' was going on.

We didn't have time to find out.

The worst 3 months of my life ended abruptly with a phone call from my mother's neighbour Celia.

…mum had died in her sleep.

I was absolutely devastated.

Both my parents had now gone…and in such a short space of time.

Losing my father so suddenly was awful, but to lose my mother so quickly afterwards too was terrible. Why did she die? This is what was puzzling me. She was in good health up to my father's passing. Then she had suddenly, and rather dramatically, worsened.

She had changed a while back when my father was taken ill. I'd noticed the rather assertive attitude which was so unlike her, but when my father died she REALLY changed. Her whole personality, mannerisms and attitude to life altered and kept altering, and it was this that was playing on my mind.

The funeral took place at the same crematorium and more or less the same people attended…including the two strangers. And they were much more talkative this time and actually approached me many times before and after the service. Their topics of conversation were of empathy and understandably rather brief but they expressed their concern for my welfare and the lady gave me her business card before they left, saying that I should contact her if I ever needed to. I never gave it a second thought as to why I would ever have the need to contact her, but I thanked them both for coming.

It turned out they were old business associates of my fathers and had lost touch over the years. They'd heard of his passing and now subsequently wanted to pay their respects when they learnt that his wife had passed away as well. I invited them to the reception afterwards but they declined saying they had to get back…to where-ever 'back' was.

At the hotel, I mingled amongst the gathering but spent most of the time talking with Celia and Tom.

The 'two foreigners' once again popped up in the conversation. Celia commented how nice they both were. "You almost felt that you knew them from somewhere," she said. I understood her feelings, especially regarding the woman, and I still sensed that they tried to keep out of everyone's way. They came across as being very kind, likeable people and were quite attentive and caring towards me. I kept making eye contact with them every now and then like before, especially the woman. I mentioned it to Celia who said that she had noticed her looking at me too!

Over the next four months I went back up to Scotland twice more to speak with the solicitors who were dealing with the selling of the house and my parents finances. They sold my father's car, and dealt with all the legalities for me. Everything else was completed by post.

I just wanted it all to be done and dusted now; including the house clearance. I had odd feelings about that as I felt like I was removing the last parts of their existence. It was nice to hold on to some of their possessions though, and I would have taken more if I had the storage space. I kept my father's old Grandfather clock, his books, an oil painting that I'd bought for my mother many years ago, and a box of old personal stuff of mine that she had been collecting over my younger years…but that was about it.

The house was snapped up quite quickly and it wasn't long before a letter arrived from the solicitors bearing a cheque for a substantial amount of money. To be honest, it was a life changing amount. I did not realise that my parents had accumulated that amount of savings. So, with the sale of the house as well…I suddenly found myself to be rather well off. It was a good feeling of financial security…but I deeply missed them both.

Wherever

"What are you doing? Are you alright?"

It was like the power switch in my mind had just been turned back on. I opened my eyes and quickly pulled myself up on the chair, grimacing for a second as I caught my left hand on something sharp, then I turned my head towards the voice. I was looking down a long corridor of an old shed. On each side were shelves laden with tins and work tools that were bathed in warm orangey red streaks of light. I could feel the heat from the sun on my face as I turned to look out of one of the dirty cobwebbed windows.

"I must have dozed off."

I got up from the old wicker chair, noticing and feeling again the pointy bit of protruding wicker and then immediately looked down at my feet. I had wellington boots on and shorts. For a second I hesitated as this didn't seem right, then I walked towards the door at the far end and opened it…

"SURPRISE!" they all said more or less together. I recognised my brother, then my sister…then my other sister, and their families. "Oh Wow," I was amazed and totally astonished. How had Avril kept this from me? I was shocked but felt elated as I looked from one face to another trying to take it all in. Everyone was laughing, probably at my expression of total bewilderment as I went to each person individually and hugged them, expressing my constant joy and amazement to each one.

"And Alec is here," said my older sister as she pointed to a man who got up from the sofa and stood in front of me. I looked at him for a moment, and then shook his hand, "it's nice to meet you Alec, thanks for coming."

Everybody laughed again as I looked around uncomfortably at everyone, searching for an understanding as to their humorous response.

"It's your COUSIN, you dumbo!" said my younger sister mockingly.

I swung back around to look at the man who was smiling but looking rather uncomfortable himself. "Alec? Oh my goodness, I'm so sorry, I didn't recognise you..." I was smiling and had my hands out in front of me in a 'please forgive me' type manner as I leaned forward and we hugged.

He spoke softly in my ear. "That's a rather nice colourful tie you're wearing," and I moved back in response to his admiration and took hold of the rather bright red and yellow striped garment in my hand.

"Yes...it IS a nice tie..." I said smiling and looking at it.

Then I looked back up at Alec. I cannot believe I didn't recognise him. Of course I knew him! And I also knew that my brother and sisters were not my REAL brother and sisters. But we always regarded each other as such. We've always been close...

I was staring…and I apologised, "Sorry…my mind was wandering there for a moment…"

"And look at those shoes!" he continued, as I looked down again and focused on the shoes that I was wearing. I stared at the fancy pointed patented style…and froze. Now I was really confused, this didn't seem right…hold on, this wasn't right! I looked back up…The sky was dark red with black storm clouds moving speedily across in a seemingly haphazard manner. I felt powerful, I felt empowered. I knew this place.

I turned to look behind me. I was alone. I turned back. There were blocks of lights in sections, huge windows of lights, one above the other…and I could see what looked like people moving around inside…yes, they were people. It was difficult to make out as they were so small, and I suddenly started to comprehend the size of everything. I was looking down upon a huge stadium type complex; the windows banking and curving forming the huge sides and then I suddenly realised how high I was.

I turned my attention to the closer surroundings. I was standing on some kind of platform. I moved forward towards the edge, and looked over. I could see soft glowing, white domes of light, arranged more or less in rows that covered the area. As I took in the immense size of it all I looked further down and closer to the platform. Almost directly below was a large rectangular area where there were no lights at all. It was black, in fact the blackest black. It was free of light and form and depth. It was a huge space of nothing. I looked back to the white domes and I could see one towards the centre of the 'arena' that was larger than the others. It was much taller and wider and its luminance seemed to be slightly pulsating. I stared; I knew about it, it meant something to me, but I could not understand the connection. I broke my focus and looked back down into the black space.

And it was just that…a black space! It was a void; a featureless rectangular area of unfathomable darkness.

I stared into the indecipherable tenebrosity.

This meant something to me too.

My thoughts were now jumbled as I battled with feelings of curiosity, yet at the same time I understood, and I had a desire to enter this blackness. Yes, I could go through. I knew it. It was an opening; it was there for me…

I looked down at the platform and took an immediate step back as I realised how close I was to the edge. Then I glanced back up to see…Alec's face…

"And you thought you were just driving home for your tea," he said with a smile. "There's a lot in store for you my boy!" he added and he laughed, as the sea of family faces joined in. And they WERE my family weren't they? Of course they were. I knew them all. I looked back at Alec. I've not seen him for years, but his face resembled the memory I had of him. No, what am I thinking…I've always known him…he's always been in my life…

I turned around and looked at everybody. They were all sitting on sofas and armchairs and all looking at me.

I suddenly felt really odd, like I was a stranger. I didn't know any of these people! I don't know any of them really, do I?

"Are you alright?" said my younger sister as I felt her hand on my arm.

I looked at her concerned but smiling face. "Yeah Ann…sorry, yeah, I'm fine…sorry, I just can't believe all this is happening." I knew her, of course I did, she was my sister, well…my stepsister…and I smiled back. I exhaled deeply. I knew everyone, they were all my family.

"Look at him" laughed my step brother… "Quick, someone get him a drink, come on…he needs some booze."

Avril walked over to me, "did you not have any idea about this? We've been organising it for months!"

Our eyes engaged, and then I caught sight of my reflection in the mirror to one side of her.

"Yep, look at you" she said as she turned to look in the mirror too…"The big six O!" Then she reassuringly squeezed my hand. "I just cannot believe you never had any idea…"

I glanced at the smiling woman looking back at me, and then switched my focus to the man whose eyes were penetrating my inner soul.

We just looked at each other.

I smiled…and I smiled back. This man was me…wasn't he?

I was suddenly disorientated again. What was going on? Who was I? Where was I? I turned my head to look directly at Avril.

Feelings of complete bewilderment and confusion filled my thoughts…

"Here we go…"

I turned towards the voice to see a smiling lad with a beard who was shielding a bottle of beer from my gaze.

"Close your eyes and have a drink. See if you can guess the brand, Dad."

I smiled and closed my eyes as I stretched out my hand…

Then the word 'DAD' registered in my brain and I quickly re-opened them…

"Are you alright?"

I was sitting on the edge of the bed and was looking at the huge TV screen in front of me. It must have cost a fortune, but it was worth every penny. "…yeah, I'm fine…I still can't get over the size of this thing!" I said smiling and pointing.

I stood up, yawned…and walked over to the patio doors. I pulled back the curtains and those annoying net curtains underneath, and then slid open the glass doors and stepped out onto the patio.

The heat hit me immediately. The temperature outside was already sweltering.

I put my hands on my hips and looked across the fields to the big white house on the horizon. I must go over one day and introduce myself to whoever lives there. You never know, the owner could be the woman of my dreams. I smiled at that thought and then I turned to see the lovely face that was looking back at me through the open patio doors. No, hold on…I'm with the woman of my dreams now. She means everything to me…

"What did you say your name was again?" I asked with an enquiring expression but followed with a huge smile. She 'rolled back her eyes' and stuck out her tongue as I turned and refocused on the rather imposing building in the distance.

"Where's Max?" I almost said under my breath.

"MAX! Come to the garden!" I shouted.

Max came gliding out of the kitchen area after a few seconds and made his way towards me. I'd walked a little way down the lawn and had turned to 'greet' him. "Max, focus on that house and its grounds please," I said pointing. I don't know why I've never thought about doing this before.

Max was an all singing all dancing high tech 'Homebot.' He's been with us for about a year now, and I've grown quite fond of him.

Max 'looked' towards the white house and the image came up on his built-in back display screen. I moved closer to view the picture. Max's optical system had an amazing focal ability and I think I could see two people. "Ooooh, that's good Max…make it bigger please," I enthused as I covered the viewer with my hands to reduce the sun glare. Max obliged and I leant closer. He had focused on the top half of a woman…who was looking back at me! Well, she wasn't, but it certainly appeared that way. Her eyes seemed fixated on mine…and then she started to smile. Was she smiling at me? That's ridiculous, I would be a dot on HER horizon, but it looked like a smile almost in recognition that she could see me…and I felt really weird.

Then suddenly Max jolted and moved quickly off to the left, making me jump with his reactive urgency, and he headed back to the house…

"Hey, Max! What're you doing? Where're you going? MAX, STOP…NOW!" I exclaimed as I watched the Homebot carry on across the lawn, onto the patio, and disappear inside the house. That was the first time he'd ever disobeyed an instruction. Max had VRC (voice recognition command), so something wasn't right.

"WHAT is going on?" I said out loud as I walked speedily towards the open patio doors to investigate his odd behaviour.

Something stopped me just before entering, and I turned and looked back across the valley.

A flash of circular colourful light immediately caught my attention high in the sky. As I focused I could see that it was a big black ball with a bright coloured fringe around its circumference that was shimmering and sparkling. I stared at it. My eyes were somehow drawn to the centre and I felt compelled to keep looking. It was a huge black circular space above the white house and I suddenly realised I was walking towards it, no…I was being pulled towards it like a magnet, though I knew I wanted to go. Was I floating? Was I off the ground? I lowered my gaze and focused on…

…the white domes.

I was looking directly down on them.

How? Was I flying?

I had no body…I was just viewing.

I felt powerful.

I felt in control.

And I was aware of a hum.

It was a constant sound and a strangely familiar one, though I could not say why. A dull, background airy noise that was inside my head. It was enhancing the strength of my thoughts. This sound was for me.

I mentally refocused and knew that I was back in my body.

Then something touched the back of my neck. I instinctively moved my hand up and turned around. It was a net curtain and I pushed it away as it enveloped my face for a moment in the breeze.

A voice called out, "…are you sure you're alright?"

I knew that voice. I adored that voice didn't I?

I was taking it all in.

I loved to do this first thing in the morning, and to take advantage of the gorgeous weather too while it lasted. The view is breath-taking and was one of the main reasons why I bought the house. I just wish my parents could see how I had invested some of the money they had left me.

I took another sip from my mug of tea and focused on the building on the horizon. It was pointed out to me by the estate agent, when I came around for the initial 'viewing,' that that was my nearest neighbour other than a mining quarry that was buried in the trees over to the right. The building was miles away; a block of white, sitting there all palatial. I owned 4 acres that spanned down into the 'valley' but apparently the white house possessed everything else that the eye could see. The owner had some connection with the quarry too.

I turned around and slowly walked back, went in through the kitchen and made my way back upstairs to the bedroom. I put the tea down on my bedside table and took hold of the bed covers to straighten them out. I noticed something on my pillow…I leaned forward…it looked like little spots of blood. Then I saw some more on the white sheet! Oh no! I immediately looked at my hands; turning them back and forth…sure enough I had a dry blood smear on the palm of my left hand. I instinctively licked it and rubbed the spot. There was a small skin tear that was slightly sore when I pushed it. Where did I get that from? I must have caught it when I was pruning and trimming trees yesterday.

I had a shower and got dressed, then looked at the sheets and pillow with the blood on. If my mother was here now she would be stripping the bed and putting on fresh pillow cases and covers. I smiled, picked up my mug, and walked downstairs.

I ran the tap in the kitchen sink and started rinsing the mug as I looked down the lawn and across at the white house…and

THEN, like a sudden rush of video playback in my head, images of my 'jaunt' appeared. I stopped still and reflected.

I had been someone else again, inside someone else's body and mind. And those domes and the huge stadium; that was all so involved, so complicated. And there was something else too, but I couldn't grasp it in my memory...

I made some cereal and took it into the living room as I was thinking, glancing at my reflection in the hall mirror as I walked through. Now THAT was me! I smiled. I was trying to keep my sense of humour with all of this.

I sat down on the edge of the sofa and glanced up at the oil painting hanging on the opposite wall. It was the painting I had given my mother many years ago. I reminisced for a moment; then thoughts of what she had written on the back of the painting came into my mind. What did she write? I put the bowl down on the coffee table and went over and took the painting off the wall and turned it over. It simply said 'From Jamie 1984' in her familiar flowing writing style. It was a picture of some flowers in a vase painted by Robert Cox. She had always liked flowers, and as I reflected on thoughts of my mother, I could remember and 'see' myself buying the painting too in an auction room. I started to get a bit nostalgic and looked over at the Grandfather clock standing by the window. This was my father's time piece or may have even been owned by my actual grandfather who I'd never met. I then glanced down at the box that sat beside the clock which had a stack of old vinyl records upon it. It was still sealed with parcel tape with my mother's hand writing again on the side that said, 'Jamie's Stuff.'

I smiled. I should really open it, but something was stopping me. It was just a funny feeling. My mother had sealed it, and I didn't want to break my mother's seal so to speak. It was as simple as that. It was a silly reason but the nostalgia of it all just prevented me from doing so. I knew what was in there anyway. It was old birthday cards, christening regalia, and other bits and bobs that she had put together over the years and it had all been presented to me on my 21st birthday. But in my mind, if I unsealed the box, it would be like I was 'undoing' the last something of her creation. I was sentimental like that. I couldn't help it. I had similar thoughts about my father too along with one that had frustrated me since his death. I'd always wondered whether he had left me a message somewhere. In fact, it was more than a wonder, it was a hope. In my early adult years, as I've said before, I had an underlying feeling that the day would come when he would sit me down and explain the wonders of my life and the reasons why I was 'different.' And because he never did, I had convinced myself that he surely must have made a plan of some sort, a plan that would have taken any unfortunate happening into consideration. But there was nothing that I could find, and boy, I had looked! My father had always been an avid reader and he had a collection of many hard and paperback books, and I had it in my mind that if he was ever going to leave a message or a note of some sort, that he would leave it in one of them. I had thumbed through the many pages, hoping that a piece of paper or an envelope addressed to me would suddenly fall out. They were sentimental hopeful thoughts that never came to fruition as I had spent a fair time checking every book for anything that might give a clue.

I placed the painting back on the wall and then picked up my cereal bowl from the table and slowly started to eat. The nostalgia had 'warmed' my mind and I was thinking about my parents.

I finished off the Weetabix, cleared up in the kitchen, and went upstairs to the bathroom to brush my teeth. I picked up my toothbrush and stopped still as I looked at it. It was a different brush AND it was red in colour. I just kept staring at it, and I actually looked up and looked away from it…and then back again. My toothbrush is blue. I don't know why, but I've always had a blue one…but this was red!

"NO!" I said out loud rather worryingly and I looked at my reassuring reflection in the mirror for a moment, then I glanced around the bathroom. No idea what I was looking for, probably for something else to look wrong as well I guess, expecting things to change. I closed my eyes, "NOOOOO!" I said again. I've got to control this. I need to be in control, I don't want it to happen…

I opened my eyes and looked at the toothbrush in my hand. It was blue! It was blue!

I walked out of the bathroom and ran down the stairs, through the hallway and into the kitchen. I glanced quickly through the window into the garden, then I turned and opened the back kitchen door and went onto the patio…and stared…at the white house. I've no idea why I did that. I just had the desire, if you will, to go outside and look across at that building. There was some connection there, I could feel it. But I don't know what.

I kept looking at the white structure sitting there in the distance, and then I walked to the edge of the patio in my bare feet and turned around to look at the back of the house. Suddenly I 'saw' the bedroom extension in my mind as memory images were triggered…and then I 'saw'

95

Max!…What was that? Some kind of a robot? And then it dawned on me…was THAT the future? Had I travelled into the future? I stood still and kept looking at the back of the house…but I wasn't seeing, I was just thinking…thinking whether I had actually lived a part of my life in a later time! That's never happened before as far as I was aware. Well, it could've done I guess but I had nothing to compare with in past jaunts. And that woman that was looking at me! Now that was very odd. Who was she? She seemed familiar somehow and was she really looking at me? Did she actually 'see' me?

I turned back around and looked over at the white house again.

There was just something about that place. I should go over there and perhaps introduce myself… "Hello, I'm your new neighbour!"

You never know, the woman of my dreams might be living there. I smiled at that thought then immediately realised that I might have had that same thought sometime before…

My life is so not straightforward at the moment.

As I started to think I looked down at the toothbrush that I was still holding!…And I smiled some more.

In the White House

That afternoon I got in my car and drove over to the other side of the valley.

I couldn't find the place at first, which was rather frustrating. It is such an imposing structure that I thought it would stand out like a beacon, drawing me in, but that was not the case. In fact I think I drove past the entrance twice, before I realised.

There was a big ornate gate that preceded the driveway and I sat in the car looking at it for a moment, wondering whether I should open it and drive down or whether I should walk. I chose the latter and drove ahead 25 yards or so to park as best I could to leave enough room for another car to get by. Mind you, I hadn't seen another vehicle on my journey over, it was that quiet around here. I'm not complaining as I love the tranquillity, and that was another one of the reasons for moving here. It is completely the opposite from living in London's hustle and bustle which, to be honest, drove me mad in the end. But sometimes I do wonder if I'm living around here totally on my own…yes, it can be THAT quiet!

I walked up to the gate. It did look impressive in its design, but it certainly hadn't been well maintained. Much of it was rusting and there were creeper type plants growing around its metalwork. I looked for a way to open it…and struggled. The sliding metal bar just did not want to…slide!

I looked through at the grass and weeds that were growing out of the higgledy-piggledy surface as the unkempt twisting driveway disappeared into a canopy of dark overhanging trees a short way ahead. I stood back. I started to wonder whether this actually was the BACK entrance instead. It definitely didn't look used.

I looked to the side of the gate at the fencing. Bits of it had broken away and I realised I could probably get through. I didn't fancy driving around again looking for the front entrance anyway…I could be here all night!

I bent down and eased my body through the gap and I was in!

I looked back and down the lane to check on my car, force of habit I guess, and then I started to make my way along the drive.

I walked through the 'archway' which was formed by the overhanging trees and as the drive swung to the right I could see that it continued on through a wood.

I stopped and hesitated for a moment, as the view somehow did not look that inviting, and I suddenly was in two minds as to whether I should actually carry on or not. I know that may sound strange, but I just felt slightly uneasy, like the feeling you get when you're lost and driving down a lane that starts to get narrower, and then you see grass growing in the middle? I think you know what I mean!

I walked on…and into the wooded area, and as I did, I suddenly heard the beginning of a low tone sound, building up to a higher tone level then almost immediately dropping back down again, then back up it went again. It was a siren…an air raid siren! NOW I felt really uneasy. An air raid siren? Had I set off some kind of elaborate house grounds alarm? I started to walk faster, then I broke into a slight jog…I don't know why, it was just a reactionary panicky thing I suppose, not knowing WHAT was going on! The sound was echoing through the trees, it was all around me…but why…what was happening? The drive turned to the left now, and I could make out something through the trees. I think there was a clearing ahead, and thankfully I could see glimpses of the white house. Good. I slowed to a walking pace and as I rounded the corner of the wall I saw them. Two thick set tall men in long black trench coats, who were urgently pushing and shoving what looked like a policeman's limp body through an open manhole in the ground. I froze in fear, as I sickeningly watched his distorted broken limbs being forcibly pushed, like a rag doll, through the narrow opening in the ground. It was a horrendous sight as his helmet suddenly took flight from his head and bounced on the deserted street. Was he dead? He was either dead or unconscious. Then suddenly the nearest man became aware of my presence and he turned towards me. His menacing piercing eyes connected with mine across the road as his rugged unshaven face magnified in front of me like an exaggerated scene from a cartoon. His suddenly raised outstretched arm aggressively pointed a finger of warning, as he shouted blaspheming words of alarm to his partner. I turned to run and heard an almost immediate ricochet explosion on the wall above me. Panic mode set in as I ran at full pelt, knowing I only had a few seconds of cover before they would sight me again. There was nowhere to hide, so I ran, ridiculously weaving from side to side, as I heard another cracking sound that split the air…

"Come on, let's cut through here!"

He said it with such confidence in his voice that I knew straight away that he'd done it before. I hesitated for a moment as I caught my breath and weighed up the situation, but I immediately followed, and so did the other three lads. We were out of sight of the following group, but I did look back to be sure.

We climbed over the stile and made our way with much hardship across the muddy field and soon entered the thankful cover of the trees in the woods. Good, I feel more at ease now. The game would have been up if we'd been seen by any of the others on the open field. We stopped and pulled chunks of sticky clinging mud from our running shoes and then we set off again, following him deeper into the trees. Schoolboy adrenalin, of doing something I should not be doing, was surging through my body. My achy tired legs had been injected with a sudden new lease of strength and power as I somehow, almost effortlessly, rode the carpet of leaves and undergrowth, with my eyes and mind focused on the way ahead, willing a familiar path or road to quickly appear.

I didn't like the uncertainty of it all. I always liked to be in control of an outcome, to be in control of a situation. But here I was, relying on this rogue, this lad, who liked to bend the rules, and who liked to bend the rules a lot! He was renowned for it, and I should've realised that he was up to something when he always recorded amazing times during cross-country events. Well, I'm in now, committed if you like, to see this through. The trouble is, he doesn't care if he gets caught, but I do. My parents would really come down on me like a ton of bricks and I certainly wouldn't hear the last of it for sure…but then, hold on…they never found out did they? They never knew…

…I tripped at pace, stumbled forward and crashed down onto the forest floor. I gathered my thoughts and pulled myself up onto my knees quickly to see where the others were, and was suddenly incredibly aware of an acute pain in my right side. I looked down to horrifyingly see blood soaking through my white T-shirt. Oh my god, what's happened? I started to shake as I nervously lifted it up to see what I had done and saw my glistening red skin that had been torn open at the waist.

"Are you alright?"

The voice startled me as I looked up into the eyes of this beautiful, enquiring but calm woman. She pulled back her wonderfully long blond shining hair that had fallen onto her perfect face, and majestically scooped it back behind her ears as she leant forward towards me.

"I'm…I'm not sure…" I slowly and hesitantly replied as I stared into her eyes, her large almond shaped deep blue eyes that seemed to be altering somehow, almost changing colour. I was transfixed. I could not move and I could not look away, and I did not want to look away, as warm thoughts and feelings flooded my mind like a cascade of everything good you could ever need. I could feel the energy; it was her energy, inside my head. She was telling me things…explaining things…a constant flow of quiet noise. I knew it was meaningful, yet it meant nothing. I knew it was important, yet I had no obvious understanding. Then her narrow lips formed a very slight smile and she raised her hand to mask my vision and I instinctively closed my eyes. I could feel her touch against my closed eyelids, against my forehead and cheeks. Her face was visible. I could still 'see' her eyes that were staring into the depths of my mind as she spoke...

"Wait for the Opening" ...the voice was soft but instructive as her face glowed beneath my eyelids. It was all I could 'see'...but slowly and gradually the blackness of my mind absorbed her like a fading image, and she disappeared.

"Look for the Opening," she said again in a soft monotone sound.

With her image gone, I was left in darkness. A black volume of space, littered with pinpoints of the dullest coloured luminance. A tightly clustered mass of the faintest colours that prevented the actual scene from being truly black.

And I WAS looking.

My eyes were moving beneath my lids against the palm and fingers of her hand, as I 'viewed' the vast open space that lay before me.

And it was space.

I was viewing millions of the tiniest, faintest, minute stars imaginable that were all joined together in one massive grid. A dimensional framework of vertical and horizontal tightly packed, almost indistinguishable dots, of barely perceptible colour...but they were colours, and they were there.

Then, I was suddenly aware of true blackness. A rectangular block of solid darkness. No dots, no colour, just a space where light, form and anything meaningful had been abolished. It was there in front of me. An oblong shape of nothingness, that I could only discern because the dots were forming its edges.

I 'stared' into the blackness, and I was aware that as I moved my eyes to view above and below it, the rectangle stayed still.

I looked deeper, hoping, wanting to find more. I stared, trying to penetrate whatever this black covering was...

And then it happened...

Right in the middle it began to appear.

An arc of light, like a crack in this windowpane of blackness.

It was so small but I could see it. A minute light source arced to form a curve, then it reduced to a point again, then it arced again with fine jagged yellow light that seemed to flash across it. It was seemingly growing, forming, coming to life as I 'stared.'

Every burst of energetic 'curving' was getting longer and getting closer to forming the complete circle...and I knew that that was the objective. It kept 'turning' then reducing, turning more, then reducing...

It was mesmerising, and I was compelled to 'watch.'

Then suddenly my mind switched 'focus' as I felt her hand lift away from my face. My eyes were still closed but my thinking had returned to my immediate surroundings. She was still there. I could sense her close to me. Should I open my eyes? I didn't want to...perhaps I couldn't?

Then a facial image started to form again. I could see it becoming clearer in my mind...

It was MY face! I was looking at ME!

"Look for the opening!" ...it was said in the same tone.

...I snapped back and 'refocused'...the circle was complete. It was now a glistening circular band of the tiniest coloured shimmering stars that appeared to be now reducing in light intensity.

As I kept 'looking' they faded quickly to merge into the millions of minute stars that now covered the space again. And then I 'saw' and realised...

That they were the fringe.

That they were the boundary.

That they were the edge and the body that contained...

The Opening!

A hole of perfect power blackness, I could 'feel' strength in its depth of indefinite existence...

...and I knew what I could do...

I got back on my feet, brushed myself down, and looked straight ahead...

...and there it was, as if it had just been magically placed before me...the white house!

I stood still and 'took in' the enormous size of the place, as the wretched siren continued to fill my ears. Now I was 'out in the open' so to speak, I was expecting to see people come running towards me. I did feel quite awkward and I wanted someone to appear quickly so I could say who I was and what I was doing here. I hurried across the gravelled frontage looking for the entrance but I could not see any doors. Then I realised that the 'drive' continued around to the right of the building and so I made my way down the side of the house as a lawn with grey statues gradually came into view. All the time I was glancing up at the windows; expecting to see concerned faces looking back at me, their eyes wondering what I was doing on their property. But there was no one...

Then 'BOOM!'

There was a huge explosion, and I cowered slightly as I stopped dead in my tracks.

'BOOM!' another one. I kept still but trying to gauge where it was coming from.

I didn't know what to do. The explosions, although seemingly loud, did seem a reasonable way off and appeared to be originating over the other side of the house. I started to walk at pace in that direction to investigate, and was soon aware that this in fact was the front of the house. The lawn was huge and gently sloped away from the frontage and as I looked across its vastness I could see my house sitting there in the far distance across the 'valley'. I smiled when I saw it. It looked so small, though I knew it was a fair size place itself. But compared with the white house, it was minute! And I was glad it was still in one piece! I scanned the area looking for any obvious reasons for the explosive noises, but there was nothing to be seen. I was suddenly aware how quiet it had become and realised the siren had stopped too.

I reverted my attention back to the white house, and viewed the stonework steps that led up to what resembled some kind of balcony which had rather tall black wrought iron railings enclosing it. As I walked, I veered out to the right slightly and I could see more steps going back down the other side too. I imagined that the front door must be up there, and as I started to climb the left hand staircase and got to the top, I could see that I imagined correctly. It was a huge oak mediaeval type door, and it was set back from the balcony under an old stone archway. It reminded me of a door that you would see fronting a castle with a moat, it was that big! I walked into the archway enclosure and looked for a method of announcing my presence. To knock on the door seemed ridiculous because of its size, but I couldn't see any other way, and so I did…and waited for 30 seconds or so. Nothing happened so I clenched my fist and thumped on the door which seemed more appropriate. Again I waited…but nothing. I then instinctively grabbed the huge door knob, turned it and pushed…and would you believe it…yes, it opened slightly…and I stopped pushing. I hesitated for a moment…and then applied more pressure to open the door, which was surprisingly easy to do, and looked inside.

I could see a huge hallway with white marble flooring, each square of which had a very pale pink colour edge to it that glowed very faintly. And in the centre of it all was a rather grand staircase that looked like it was constructed out of white marble too.

I stepped inside and called out…

"Hello…is there anybody here?"

I paused for 5 seconds or so just listening…then… "Can anybody hear me? Hello!" I said again.

Nothing.

Just complete silence, except for my voice echoing around the walls. It was a massive space.

I took a few more steps and ventured inside a bit further. There were quite a few doors that I could see to the left and right of the staircase, and the hall seemed to go a long way back. I tentatively moved to one side and leaned to look past the staircase, really to see if I could see anybody, and it DID go a long way back. It narrowed into a corridor that looked ridiculously long. It was almost like an optical illusion, I honestly couldn't see the end properly.

I looked back to the white marbled staircase. It was very wide at the base and then narrowed as it went up, parting into two towards the top, one set going right, the other to the left...an amazing sight.

"Hello!" I said awkwardly again.

Everything seemed so huge. I looked at the walls, and then up to the ceiling. They actually looked like they were made of glass, and there were coloured shapes with swirling patterns that seemed to be inside the glass...it was very strange. There were no pictures, no windows, and no furniture of any sort. It was just big and empty. But it somehow felt lived in. It was so perfectly clean and bright...and yet, there were no lights! I suddenly realised that the whole hall was perfectly lit, but I couldn't see any light source. There was no grand chandelier hanging down in the centre and there were no standard lamps or wall lights'. But the whole hall and staircase seemed perfectly illuminated.

"Helloooooooooo!" I said again, as I kept scanning the hall and made my way over gingerly to one of the doors on the right. There's got to be someone here somewhere...

My intention was to knock on the door, but as I moved closer, an array of coloured lights suddenly filled my vision. I could see illuminated panels of different sizes, shapes and depths, and some were changing colour. It was incredible. I stopped still and just looked. It was like a new room had suddenly appeared from nowhere, though I immediately knew this was not just a room. It was more a centre, an area of control.

I took a step back and the door reappeared and the banks of coloured lights vanished. The wall was solid once more.

I was feeling different. I was tuning in. More information was being released to me.

I was safe and somehow I felt protected.

I turned and looked at the staircase. If I had a big enough house to accommodate one, this would've been the style I would've chosen. It was perfect...

Legitimate Thinking

Should I fry or grill?

I'll be healthy and grill.

Bacon sandwiches, mmm you can't beat it.

I turned on the grill and went over to open the fridge door…and stopped dead in my tracks.

The door!

The white house!

How did I get back? I cannot remember driving back!

I hurriedly walked through to the hallway and saw my car keys hanging on the hook. I opened the front door and sure enough there was my car on the drive. I closed the door slowly and walked back through into the kitchen. I looked up at the clock. It had just gone 5.30 p.m. I cannot remember what time it was when I went over there, but it must have been around mid-afternoon, so the time now is nothing out of the ordinary. I sat down at the kitchen table and cupped my hands around my mug of tea and pondered.

Something must have happened over at the white house. I closed my eyes…I can remember the coloured lights in the room and the staircase. I saw the blond-haired woman didn't I? She knows so much about everything and she showed me around her house. It's so much larger than I thought, with many different rooms, but we didn't go anywhere did we? I just viewed.

And that was her in the forest when I fell. She helped me! She stopped the bleeding!

I opened my eyes and stared straight ahead in realisation. It was her!

Had she prevented me from possibly bleeding to death? I may be exaggerating, but she had certainly helped me…I just knew.

I quickly pulled up my t-shirt and looked at the scar on my right side…

When my father took me to hospital after the fall, the doctors didn't believe I had cut myself by just falling on something. I remember the commotion that it caused as they said that they were obliged to involve the Police because they suspected that I had been shot. Of course, I was totally oblivious to anything of the kind as were my school friends that I was with at the time. I remember my father having to sort it all out because it became quite a fuss, although I did become a bit of a minor 'celebrity'.

And NOW it all makes sense. I HAD been shot, by one of those two shady men in the street who were disposing of that body! But how? I mean, HOW did I get hurt like that in one jaunt and carry it over to another? And the time factor! That happened when I was young didn't it? And why do I have no recollection of the two shady men connection until now?

I looked at my mug, and then quickly looked over at the grill. The bacon! I got up and went over and pulled out the tray. Mmmm, the two rashers of cooked bacon smelt superb and I opened the bread bin to butter a couple of slices. I stopped as I opened the butter dish…

I didn't put the bacon under the grill did I? I was going to do it…but I didn't do it. I know I didn't do it!

I slowly buttered the bread as I thought about it. It may sound trivial, considering everything else that has been going on lately, but it reminded me of the one thing that my father used to say to me to 'explain' why I was different. And I use the word 'explain' rather loosely. He would always use the comparison of driving along in your car thinking about something and then you suddenly realise that you cannot remember driving the last mile or so. The subconscious mind was driving whilst the conscious mind was thinking.

"The mind is the universe," he would always say.

It was his 'answer' to most of the strange things that ever happened to me. It was always his passing shot across the bows as he sailed off over the horizon. And that's how I remember it; I never dwelt upon it. Perhaps I should have done, because now, it seems to make more sense, and I don't just mean whether I put the bacon under the grill subconsciously or not, or how I got this mug of tea, because I don't consciously remember making that either. No, it's the big picture. It's what I know now, and I do know much more. I know that when I am in control I will be powerful. I will consciously be able to delve into the multi-dimensional facets of my mind and be anyone, be anywhere and at any given time!

I don't know why…but I just know.

Lifetime Chase

I woke up the next day knowing that I had to get back over to the white house.

I had breakfast and got ready to go.

I grabbed my car keys and went out the back way through the kitchen, out onto the patio and looked across the valley. There it was in the distance. This white propitious structure; sitting there all nonchalant and carefree. But I knew now that it had meaning, it was significant…and I think I always did know.

I locked the kitchen door, walked across the patio and started making my way down the side of the house. As I did, I stopped. There was someone on my drive! I hadn't seen them, or heard them…I just knew.

There were a lot of bushes and trees to the left of the house which I called my 'secret garden' and I cautiously ran quickly into there and ducked down. I then moved slowly towards the front of the house behind the cover of the bushes. I was almost crawling as I saw my car with two men standing beside it. I stopped still, holding my breath. These were not delivery drivers or postmen or anyone casual, they were official looking people. I watched them as they surveyed my car then the front of my house. One of them walked towards me and I lowered myself further, and I glanced up at him as he walked past, catching sight of his face as he made his way down the side to the back garden. My heart started to race, he looked decidedly like one of the men in the trench coats that fired a gun at me. I couldn't be sure, but there was something about his deep set eyes and his body language that made me draw a comparison.

I was now kneeling and stooping low. I watched the other man. He stood perfectly still looking at my front door. I looked to the right down the side path. The other man had disappeared around the back. My heart continued to pound. I looked down at the grass and lowered myself further, and then the other man reappeared and walked past me again and back to the front. I glimpsed his face again. It was enough for me to confirm to myself that it was him. This must be the trench coat pair.

I could barely see them through the foliage of the bushes, but I could make out enough to see what they were doing…which was not a lot. They both just stood there, and I couldn't hear any talking.

It seemed ages until I was aware that they were walking back up the drive to the lane. I raised my head slightly for a better view to see them exiting left and out of my eye line. I dropped back down again and strained my ears to listen. Sure enough, after about 5 seconds I heard two car doors shut. I waited for the engine to start…

It didn't.

I knelt back up and thought of my options. It was either to go back into the house and hope that they go away? Or, to get into my car and drive like a bat out of hell to get away from them? I pondered on the two options. There were probably others of course, but what sprang to mind were just those two. I went with the 'bat out of hell' and started to move to a bush closer to my car. I didn't want to hang around for the trench coat twosome to get angry!

The front hedge was tall; there was no way they could see me on the drive now, but I just wanted to be sure. I stooped forward and ran across to the side of my car and gently put the key in the lock and turned. It unlocked and I quietly opened the door and got in. I always left the car facing the lane. It was just a habit thing, and just as well.

Right, here we go...I put the ignition key in and then looked up at the end of the drive. There was no sign of any movement as I hesitated for a moment...then turned the key. The engine sprang into life as I immediately shoved it into first gear, pulled the door shut, and accelerated down the drive. I got to the end, slowed slightly to exit right, as I looked left. There was nothing there. I put my foot down and looked in the rear view mirror...nothing! There was no car following. I looked quickly forward with the bend approaching. Perhaps they had tricked me somehow; were they around the corner? My adrenalin was pumping as I took the bend...and then out of it...no, it was clear. I kept looking in the mirror, expecting a car to suddenly appear, but no. I kept driving and made my way over the valley to the white house.

Although they had done nothing untoward, I just knew that the situation would have developed into something not to my liking if I had shown myself. They were after me and I don't think a simple chat was part of their agenda. If they were the trench coated pair, could they have been 'following' me since I was at school? Could they be time travellers? Now that all sounds ridiculous and very far-fetched, but there's no easy explanation.

I parked my car at the same spot in the lane and made my way along the tried route as before. There was still not a soul to be seen as I walked down the side and around to the front of the building. I stopped again to look over at my house sitting there in the far distance. I stared, almost expecting to see something happening. Mind you, a pair of binoculars would be needed as it was just a structure on the horizon.

I turned and walked towards the first lot of steps and started to climb. When I got to the top I turned left and I was facing the massive door again. I don't know why, but I looked for a knocker or a bell once more and then I fist thumped it like I did last time. I waited a few seconds just in case, and then I turned the huge door knob and pushed. Sure enough, it opened slightly and I pushed it further to view inside…and was immediately shocked!

Everything was different. The floor, the walls, even the staircase. I just stood still and scanned the very dimly lit view that lay before me. It looked like how it should look in this sort of building if you know what I mean, but not what I saw yesterday. It had a dark wooden floor that was partially covered with an old fashioned dull red patterned carpet. The walls were of dark wood too, and I could see framed paintings that were being illuminated by wall lights set above each one.

"Hellooooo, is there anybody here? Hello."

I ventured a little more inside and immediately smelt the 'oldness' of the place. The staircase was again of dark wood and had two large, strange humanoid figurines that 'guarded' the steps on either side. They seemed to mould into the staircase; their elongated heads looking a bit disproportionate in size to their bodies. My eyes were now beginning to adjust to the rather dim interior and I walked further in and looked up the staircase. "Hello…hellooooo!" I called out again. There were two lights on the wall at the top of the stairs that illuminated a huge painting. I walked closer to the staircase. It was of a rather attractive older looking woman and I could just make out the top half of her body. Her face was the most 'stand out' in the picture and her eyes looked almost alive and were really captivating. I walked up two stairs and called out again, "Hello, I'm from across the valley…anyone here?"

I waited and listened…my line of vision focused on the face in the painting. But again there was nothing to hear and so I slowly started to walk up the stairs. Each step creaked as I tentatively made my way upwards, holding on to the left banister. I was looking at her face or more her eyes really. It was as if she was looking at me constantly and I was reciprocating.

When I got to the top I looked left and right. I couldn't see any doors. I walked to the left as far as it went which was about 20 feet. There was another light on the wall, but no door or anyway through. I walked back and passed the painting to the other end. There was another wall light, but again strangely no thoroughfare. This was so odd.

I walked back to the huge full length painting of this mesmerising woman. She was so lifelike, so real, and triggers were activating thoughts in my mind that I knew her. The majestic splendour of her full length dark robe seemed to sparkle as I moved my eyes. The painting looked old with its matt gold, intricate ornate weathered framework, but I somehow knew that it was not. I stretched out my hand and touched the 'canvas.' It felt strangely warm and was smooth like glass. A completely different feel to how it appeared. I glanced up at her face. She was looking down at me. She couldn't be, but it seemed that way. I stepped back towards the stairs, still looking at her kind facial expression, then stepped forward again and placed my hand on her 'robe'. It most definitely was not a painting. The warmth from the smooth surface seemed to surge into my hand and up my arm. I could feel my brain tingling as it received this inner energy. I withdrew my hand and the feeling persisted for a few seconds then faded. I felt quite strange, almost disorientated as I turned and walked back down the stairs and then around to the left at the bottom. My mind properly 'focused' as I looked to the back of the hall. I could see various wall lights, but no doors or windows. It was just a massive space with one way in and one way out as far as I could determine. I went around to the other side of the stairs and looked down towards the back. Again, I could see no openings, no doorways, no exits. I looked back at the door. It was comforting to see that it was still slightly open. Then I walked over to the nearest painting on the wall. It was one of about 10 that were all more or less in a row, set just below my eye level, each with a wall light above highlighting the work.

It was a still life picture of flowers in a bowl in a very ornate frame and as I looked at it I glanced along to the next painting and the next and the next…and I realised they were all the same! I also realised that it resembled the painting that I bought for my mother many moons ago. I reached out and gently felt the surface. Again it was smooth and glass-like and warm to the touch. This was weird.

I didn't know what to make of all this, and why is it all so different from last time? I looked up towards the ceiling and I was immediately aware that I couldn't actually make it out…it was so dark…and then, as my eyes focused properly, I saw a few very small white lights…Wow! They looked like stars. I kept looking upward, as I moved my head to the left, then to the right. My goodness, it was like looking at the night sky. I could now see hundreds of stars stretching right to the back of the hall; in fact I could not see a true divisional end. It was absolutely amazing. My mouth dropped open as I took in this incredible sight…and it wasn't flat, it had depth and I knew this depth was infinite.

'BANG'! it was a heavy thud type sound and I knew immediately that it was the huge front door closing, and boy was that a sudden wake up call. I ran towards the front entrance in a panic. An instant 'shut-in' feeling took over as I grabbed the large door knob, twisted it and pulled at it with force. It opened, and as the pleasing light of the day quickly hit my eyes, I immediately saw two men shaped silhouettes standing before me…then felt a sharp pain in my neck…

Different Hospital

I opened my eyes. I was lying on my left side and feeling woozy as I blinked to focus on 3 TV monitors. I raised my head up slightly to see what looked like images of brains on each screen. I propped myself up more. I was in some kind of hospital ward. There were 6 or 7 beds over the other side of a rather large medical room. They were all unoccupied and each one had hospital type fancy instruments alongside. Then a voice softly said, "Don't worry, lay back down, you need your sleep," and as I turned my head towards the sound I briefly focused on a bespectacled woman with long blond hair, who was wearing a blue type of uniform, before I 'dropped off' again.

When I opened my eyes next, I was almost in a sitting up position in bed as I started to focus on my surroundings. I was in some kind of cubicle. What was going on? Where was I? My head hurt, that's one thing for sure. I still felt woozy, but I felt more awake.

Everything seemed bright which made me blink a few times as I adjusted to the conditions. I was in a small white walled room with an open doorway directly ahead. I tried to move. My arms felt like lead. I could move them about an inch or so but that was about it; the same with my legs. It felt like I was being restrained, but I could see that I wasn't. I realised I was wearing some kind of skin tight grey patterned body tunic. I could see the covering on my arms and chest and I had a white sheet over the lower half of my body up to my waist. I tried to move again, but I just couldn't. I looked at my arms. There was nothing holding me down, but it was impossible to move. I looked up at the ceiling and noticed a small round black dome in the middle. I then heard footsteps approaching and I immediately turned my attention to the doorway.

In walked three people, a man and two women all dressed in white medical outfits. They stood in line looking at me. "How are you feeling today?" enquired the man in an American accent. He was in his late 50s, with short dark hair, dark complexion and a hard chiselled face. He gave the impression that he was in charge.

I felt strange. I could feel my mind was taking longer to process thoughts. "Why am I here? What's going on?" I responded.

"You were involved in a motorcycle accident. I would say you're very lucky to be alive, it could've been fatal." He replied.

"What?…I don't remember anything about that…"

I was trying to think back, what I was doing? Where I was going? I just couldn't think straight, though a motorbike crash did sort of make sense somehow…

"Don't worry, you're going to be OK, we need to do further tests though, but you're in good hands." He looked at his two colleagues for their approval which he dutifully received with nodding heads and smiles.

I was slowly nodding my head too in thankful agreement as I stared into mid-air trying to search in my mind for answers.

"My name is Dr Graham, and this is Dr Michaels and Dr Keifer," he announced as he pointed with his open hand. "We've been looking after you."

"Well, thank you…how long have I been here then?" I asked, "And why can't I move?"

"You've been unconscious for a few days, and don't worry, your limb paralysis is temporary like your memory, and will return soon." He paused and smiled… "I'll get some breakfast sent through to you…and it's good to see you awake."

He then turned and they all walked out through the doorway leaving me absolutely dumbfounded. I just could not remember anything about ANYTHING! I attempted to search my mind for information.

I could not do it. My mind felt lazy. It would not connect as such with the right internal mechanism. I started to think more about the accident. What accident? This was very frustrating.

I tried to move my arms again. Literally an inch upwards, that was about it, though I could feel my muscles attempting to do more.

"Hi there, my name is Anna, and look what I've got for you!" came another American voice.

She glided in and placed a tray in front of me that connected somehow to the sides of the bed.

I looked down at what had been presented…a bowl of two Weetabix and milk and a slice of toast and jam. I looked back up at this happy, smiling woman as her eyes connected with mine. She was in her late 20s early 30s, with dark straight shoulder length hair and was dressed in a dark blue one piece body suit that fitted right up to her neck with a lighter blue waist belt that fitted such as to show off her shapely body.

"I'll feed you, so don't concern yourself," she continued as she positioned herself beside me.

I felt hopeless. What on earth is going on? Here I am, propped up in bed, not able to move, and being spoon fed like a baby, by this rather attractive woman.

"I'm sorry about this," I said to her in between mouthfuls.

"Don't be silly, that's what I'm here for," she responded as she cut another piece of cereal off with the spoon.

I started to feel sad, really forlorn. I was completely lost in my mind as to what was happening, what had happened, and what was going to happen.

My eyes started to well up…which was VERY unlike me.

She reacted, "Hey, come on…don't do the crying thing on me now…"

She put down the spoon and pulled a cloth from her pocket and wiped my eyes.

Goodness me, I cannot remember the last time I felt like this. It washed over me so quickly…

"I'm sorry," I said again, as I fought to control my emotions.

"Stop apologising," she continued, "It's quite natural to feel the way that you do…you've been through a lot."

"Have I?" I responded frustratingly, as I composed myself rather rapidly and looked at her, "Well, I'll have to take your word for it…"

She looked back at me with a slight smile, opened her mouth as if to speak; paused…then she spoke in a hushed tone as she leaned closer, "You've got a lot to look forward to…"

"How is the new patient?" said yet another American voice rather loudly as Anna pulled back rather swiftly. I looked over to the doorway to see a short woman with dark cropped hair, dressed the same as Anna, standing there.

"He's doing fine," replied Anna as she raised another spoonful towards my mouth.

"Good…good" continued the new lady, "once you've finished off here, come and find me." Then she gave me a quick glance and disappeared out of the room as quickly as she had arrived.

I looked at Anna with an expression of uncertainty. She smiled, "don't worry; I'm the one looking after you." They were comforting words indeed for the worrying situation that I had found myself in. I liked Anna.

Later that day I was wheeled through into another room and was positioned under a large metallic dome shaped instrument that was 'scanning my injuries' to check progress. I saw the 3 doctors who were keen to administer painkillers regularly and they explained that the grey bodysuit I was wearing 'insured correct bone and ligament alignment during the healing process.'

I was comfortable with it all; well, as comfortable as I could be considering the situation, though going to the toilet and general hygiene was far from comfortable and very embarrassing to say the least. But it's like anything new, it can be difficult at the beginning, but after a while, when routine sets in, it becomes less of a concern. And that's what happened over the next few days. With Anna's positive outlook, reassurance and assistance, I was adapting to my new unfortunate predicament and my mind didn't feel so 'fuzzed' though I still could tell things were not right.

"Can you remember the accident now?" she asked as she placed a mug of tea on my tray in front of me.

"I think I can…I can remember bits anyway…not very clear though…"

"Will this put you off riding again, or will you be just as keen d'you think?" she asked with a knowing smile as she offered the mug to my lips.

I smiled back, "once a biker always a biker, that's what they say don't they?" …I paused as I took a sip, and then I continued reflectively, "…actually, I'm not really sure…"

"Hey, let's get you back on your feet first…take one step at a time," she interjected.

"…Did you have a motorcycle when you lived with your parents?" she continued…

"Yes…yes I did, well, a motor scooter anyway…I've always had bikes."

"Did your father mind? I mean, wasn't he a bit concerned?"

"I think he used to ride bikes when he was younger too…so…"

"Oh I see, like father like son then…what did he do for a living?"

I hesitated…for a moment I couldn't remember… "I think he used to work for different companies, giving advice on structuring their businesses and things like that."

To be honest, I never knew exactly what my father did as a job. He would go to work in the morning, and come home in the evening. Sometimes he would be away for days at a time too, and I certainly cannot remember him ever discussing anything about it. Perhaps he did, but I cannot remember.

"Well, I've got a surprise for you...are you ready?" she smiled as she put the mug down on the tray and lent forward towards me on her chair.

I'd only known Anna a short time, but I'd already grown quite fond of her. She was very caring and seemed to be on my wavelength too which was really nice. I looked at her with a coy puzzled look on my face. I thought for a moment that she was going to present me with a gift...

"So are you? Are you ready?" she jokingly insisted again, her eyes widening.

"Yesssss, yes I am." I replied, smiling.

She leant forward a bit more...

"Well...your father...used to work for us!"

I stared at Anna for a moment, "What?" I was absolutely taken aback.

She was nodding her head and her expression had turned slightly more serious.

"Yes, I never met him, but I know that he was well respected. He carried out important work."

"What, for the hospital?" I asked, perplexed.

Anna paused.

"...This hospital is just part of a much bigger organisation. Your father was involved with the other side of it all."

"So what did he do?" ...I felt really strange asking her that, almost awkward. He was my father; I should know more about him than she did for goodness sake. But to hear him being mentioned was also quite overwhelming in the situation I found myself in, and after all this time too. I felt very comforted. It was as if he was still alive, but it did feel very odd.

"He worked on projects for the government. Dr Graham used to know him, he'll have a word with you when he's 'on his rounds' later I'm sure."

"He used to know him!" I blurted out.

This is crazy! Here I am laying in a hospital bed somewhere in deepest Somerset and we're talking about my father like he was once part of the furniture.

"I know, it must seem very strange suddenly hearing your father being mentioned like this, but it's true…and he was greatly respected and I know he was particularly missed by my colleagues at the time when he retired."

I realised I had my mouth gaping open and I quickly closed it. My father worked for the government…and doing what?

Dr Graham, accompanied by Dr Michaels and Dr Keifer suddenly walked in. Anna responded by standing up straight away, "Thank you Anna," said Dr Graham. Anna nodded and left the room.

"…and how are you feeling this evening, Jamie?" he asked as he turned his attention towards me.

I responded quite quickly, but I did take note of the use of my name for the first time, as I'm sure I hadn't heard it used before.

"I'm getting there I think, thanks…and I can't believe it, but I hear that you knew my father?"

"Yes I did, yes…I certainly did," he replied as he gesticulated towards the vacant chair beside my bed. I nodded…

"Can I just say that I'm quite confused with all this," I continued... "how has all this happened, I mean...you know my name, you know my father...and where exactly are we? This doesn't feel like a normal hospital to me...and everyone is American, not that I'm complaining of course..."

The two other doctors excused themselves and walked out as he smiled and sat down beside me on the chair and slowly breathed in...and exhaled...

"You're in a hospital wing of a military base on the outskirts of Dallas."

"DALLAS!" I said astounded, "Dallas in Texas...in America?"

"That's the one," replied Dr Graham, smiling again... "Let me explain..."

"How? Why...why am I here?" I said, interrupting him.

"Let me explain Jamie...we had an agreement with your father, that if anything serious happened to you, and I mean serious as in life threatening, you would be treated in your homeland...and so here you are. It was your father's wish..."

I stared at Dr Graham...my expression one of total bewilderment.

"Your father worked for us...and he built up a strong reputation with his dedication and his particular skills. Now, I know you are not aware of any of this, and I'm sorry that you have to find out whilst you're recuperating in a hospital bed too..." Dr Graham paused...

"He worked on top secret projects that no one outside his work circle could know about and that really did mean no one, including family. He was sworn to secrecy for life, Jamie...so don't feel badly towards him that he kept you in the dark. He had no choice...he had to."

Dr Graham paused again and looked directly into my eyes. I was absolutely perplexed. I just lay there returning the stare, my mouth unfortunately gaping again with puzzlement and confusion.

"...your father told us a lot about you when you were growing up..."

"Really?" I said with a screwed up face and eyes. I just couldn't believe what I was hearing. This was all so surreal.

"Yes...really!" he said as he slowly nodded his head. "We know that you are in possession of a great ability...and we want you to make use of it with us...and for us..."

My parents were the only people who ever knew about my so-called abilities, and to hear it like this from a complete stranger was very different indeed. I know it may sound a bit conceited, but it did make me feel special...

"...and I should add, you'll be paid for your services of course, and quite handsomely too if I may say so...but we need something else from you in return...and that is commitment. Like your father, you will need to sign official government papers that will prevent you from disclosing what you see, hear, learn and do...to anyone...forever! It's a serious engagement that would restrict your freedom of action, and so, it's not for everyone...but YOU are not just anyone; you are your father's son, and you have the qualities to go far within the organisation like he did."

I lay there looking at him. This all didn't seem real. I'm lying paralysed in a hospital bed in my hometown Dallas, and have been told that I'm 'lucky to be alive' one minute, and then being propositioned about some secret job for the government the next. And to top that, it's all to do with my father...who used to WORK for them?

I tried to take stock of the situation I was in, but I just could not think straight…I still felt woozy and as I said, my mind was lazy and slow and everything else was happening in 'fast forward' mode. I couldn't fathom it all out…

"I don't feel the same in my mind as I used to, I really don't…and you're saying all this to me, hoping that I'm going to recover, but I still cannot move…and I may not ever be able to, even though you say it's temporary, you can't know for sure can you…"

His expression altered from serious and official to one of reassurance, "Look, your latest test results are telling me that your muscles and ligaments are healing nicely and you will have good movement again. We'll be able to take the medical suit off soon, possibly tomorrow, but please refrain from attempting to move at the moment. Just be patient, you're almost there. And the way you feel mentally is definitely due to your medication. You will be your normal self once that is finished…so Jamie, do not concern yourself…you ARE going to fully recover!"

Again, I just looked at him. I was absolutely astonished with everything that was being said to me, and I'm sorry to mention my mind again, but I just knew that I was not processing the information that was being presented to me in the way that I normally do.

"Well, I'm grateful for all that you and everybody here are doing to help me. I think this is the first time I've ever had to stay in hospital as far as I can remember" (and that wasn't very far).

"…and what you're proposing sounds intriguing but…it is not sinking in at the moment, I think I need to ask you more questions and…"

"Let's see how things are tomorrow…" interrupted Dr Graham in a kind but almost condescending way, "…we've been easing back on your medication, so you should be more 'with it' in the morning. It will give you time to digest what I have said and I can fill in the gaps then if you like…"

I agreed. And I DID like. It all sounded quite fascinating and very mysterious, especially with the involvement of my father; …I found that part incredible. All my life I always thought he was 'holding back' on me, but I never thought it would be connected with something of this nature. It really does come over as if he was some kind of secret agent or spy.

After about a minute of Dr Graham leaving, Anna walked in with a glass of water in one hand and a tablet in the other. She was a lovely distraction on the eye and the mind…

"So…lots of food for thought then," she said as she walked around the bed and sat down on the chair next to me. That expression really didn't sound right coming out of her mouth in her American accent and it made me smile. I breathed in and exhaled, puffing my cheeks, "Yep, certainly is a lot to take in…and I still cannot believe that my father was involved in all this and I also cannot believe I'm in America! Mind you, I should've put two and two together with all the accents."

"Yep, it's all happening," she said smiling… "And you should be proud of him…he did a lot for the organisation." She leant forward and placed the tablet in my mouth then offered the glass to my lips. "…and this is your last bit of medication, you should be feeling oh so much better tomorrow."

I swallowed the tablet. Good, I'd been taking tablets for England over the past few days, or should I say, America.

She held the glass in her hand and just looked at me. I returned the stare and smiled… "Come on, what do you know Anna? Tell me what you know about what my father did. Tell me anything…"

She hesitated for a bit… "It was all top secret work Jamie. I cannot say anything until you're 'on board' so to speak. But what I will say is that it would be an honour to work with you. It's in your blood…though you didn't know it…" she laughed and then added, "…You've got a lot to look forward to."

…I remember her saying that to me days ago.

"Let's wait until tomorrow, like Dr Graham said," she continued, "sleep on it as they say."

I wondered how Anna knew that Dr Graham had said that as she wasn't in the room at the time…but I didn't dwell on it.

Official Decision

The next morning I awoke to find I was free of the medical suit. I cannot remember it being removed…but it had gone, and I felt really well. I pulled my arms up and stretched them out. Wow, that was good.

"Go steady, no big steps yet." Said Anna as she walked in through the doorway.

"Look!" I satisfyingly announced, "look…I can move them!"

She came around to the side of me with an orange juice and a slice of toast on a tray and attached it to my bed. "Now be careful, and see if you can take the toast."

I knew I could. My arms, body, everything, felt fine. I pulled myself up further and took the toast from the plate. "Thank you," I said as I bit into it with relish. "My goodness I'm so pleased…I feel…I feel quite normal," I added as I chomped away.

She smiled at my description, "Good, I'm pleased too. But take it slowly, it looks good, but you don't want to undo anything by doing something silly."

She was right. I am a bit gung-ho sometimes, but it was lovely to feel like this…and my brain was working at full capacity. That may sound a strange way to describe it, but I could just tell that everything was back to normal.

"What happened to the medical suit then? I woke up, and it was gone..." I asked as I took a sip of the orange juice.

"The night team doctors removed it. You were fast asleep. They said they would try to do it without disturbing you...and they did."

"Why didn't they wait until now, or at least when I was awake?" I asked.

"Don't worry about it, it's done Jamie. They must have had their reasons. Anyway, it's so good to see you moving freely...but like I say, you mustn't do too much too soon"

Anna was a lovely woman and I did feel very comfortable having her around me.

"So!" she said questionably... "Have you come to a decision? Will you be working with me or not working with me?" she said with a huge smile on her face.

I must be honest; she had me under her spell. My heart was almost ruling my head, which was totally against motherly advice of course. But in saying that, I knew that if I agreed, it would change my life forever by the sound of things. And knowing that my father had intentionally put my name forward; well, it was almost like he wanted me to be involved.

"I need to find out more, but...yes, I'm probably going to agree."

She was standing a good 6 feet away from me and almost ran towards me to give me a kiss on the cheek. "I'm really pleased, Jamie," she said, then she walked backwards to almost return to the same spot.

"Are you alright?" I asked… "You seem on edge…what's wrong?"

She hesitated for a moment then replied, "I know you can read thoughts…I just, well…I just don't want you reading mine," then she gave a coy smile.

"Anna…you've nothing to worry about there," and I smiled. "My mind has moved on, it's altered, that was a passing phase…like my adolescence," and I laughed… "I cannot do it now, consciously or subconsciously. I don't know how I know that…I just do."

Anna must know a lot about me that she's not saying either. I guess it's all from the doctors and what they learnt from my father. It just makes me think though that my father must have known so much about me. He knew how I was going to develop, so why didn't he ever tell me or at least hint how it was all going to turn out. I still cannot fathom out how my mother and myself didn't know about all this secret government work that he was doing though. But then I guess the clue is in the word 'secret.'

"Can I get up now? I've had enough of this bed." And I really had. Even when they took me for the various tests I was wheeled out in the thing.

"Could you stay put just for a while longer, I know Dr Graham will be in soon, and I'm sure he'll be pleased with what you're going to tell him."

"OK, and I'll be glad to get my normal clothes back on too." I was wearing just a pair of shorts under the bed sheet.

In walked Dr Graham and on his own this time. "Good morning, you're looking well, Jamie…and thank you Anna!" It was a dismissive thank you again, and she reacted with a nod of the head, though she gave me a quick smile as she walked out.

"I feel...like a million dollars!" I responded, knowing it would make him smile.

He laughed, "It's good to hear. Well you certainly have made an excellent recovery. You'll find no scars or blemishes or anything untoward left on your body. It's been a success...and how do you feel in your mind? Clearer? More active...?"

He was asking the questions but I'm sure he was saying it knowing what the answers would be anyway.

"I feel back to normal, I really do...Everything seems to be OK."

It might have been something to do with the medication reduction I suppose, but I certainly just wanted to get out of bed and get moving again.

"Good, and have you given some thought to what we spoke about yesterday?" he asked in a disguised nonchalant manner with eyes enlarged and his eyebrows raised. I knew that he was desperate to ask me, and I think in his mind he was thinking it would just be a formality. I suddenly felt in control of the situation, and the mischievous side of me was bubbling up for the first time in a while...

"What if I say NO? I mean, I need to know more really, like what I'd actually be doing, would I be away from home a lot and things like that...?"

He made a noise with his mouth by folding his lips inwards, then he looked at me intently, "...If you say YES...you would leave your mundane, routine life behind and you would move into a world that very few people would have the opportunity to experience. It's that big Jamie. But I

135

cannot give you any more information unless you commit, it's as simple as that."

"And when you say, commit?" I asked, with MY eyes enlarged and eyebrows raised.

He pulled up the chair and sat down. "...It's like I said yesterday...It's a lifetime engagement. Once you're in you're in and there's no turning back. I know I said I'll fill in the gaps...and I will; I'll show you around the complex, you'll meet everyone, I'll answer anything you want to know, and I'll tell you what we want you to do...but first you need to read the contract. And once you have and you are agreeable to it, you must sign it, and commit."

I listened to his words. It was serious stuff indeed, and I knew I shouldn't take this half-heartedly, but what had I to lose? The one thing going through my mind was my father's participation in all of this. That I would be working on something that he had been involved with, and that he 'saw' me being involved with too.

"May I see the contract then?"

"Good, excellent," said Dr Graham. "Anna will come back and escort you to the restroom to get cleaned up; then we'll sit down together and we can go through the details."

I was slightly wobbly on my feet when I got out of bed but otherwise I was fine. It was so good to be walking around once more.

Anna led me down a different corridor; presented me with a towel, 'clothing' and an 'id tag' that I had to 'show' the sliding door when I wanted to come out, and she waited for me outside.

The 'clothing' was another body type suit but in a non-patterned, plain grey colour. It was more like Anna's than the medical one that I had to wear before. And as I put it on it almost seemed to form around my body, but not tight. The wrists banded parts were strange as they did actually tighten slightly after I pushed my hands through. There were no fasteners or zips; it just seemed to attach to me.

Once ready, I walked through the sliding doorway to be met by Anna who made a comment on my 'excellent dress sense' and then we went down the corridor to another door which slid open and she beckoned me to go through.

Dr Graham and the two other doctors were sitting facing me around a large oval glass table. "Thank you Anna," said Dr Graham, and as I turned to look back at her, she'd already gone and the door had practically closed.

"Please, please…come forward, take a seat."

I walked towards the table which was quite high off the ground and I realised that they were sitting on tall white plastic looking chairs, like bar stools. I positioned myself on the one awaiting me.

"You remember Dr Michaels and Dr Keifer…" he said gesticulating towards them. "Good morning," they both said almost in unison, and I reciprocated. I then looked down at the glass table top which was alive with colour and shapes that seemed to be moving slowly in lines within the material. I looked up at Dr Graham, and as I did the door slid open behind me again and I turned to see two military gentlemen walk in and they positioned themselves, hands behind their backs, either side of the doctors.

"…and this is General Varnes," said Dr Graham pointing with his hand again, "and General Grogan."

They both tipped their heads forward very slightly and quickly in polite recognition as I started to gauge the seriousness of what was going on. Generals? I didn't understand military ranks but I knew that a General was pretty high up.

"They are both here to confirm your understanding of the agreement and to witness your signing and commitment," he continued.

I nodded my head.

The whole tone felt different now and I must admit I didn't feel comfortable.

The contract was offered to me in audio or written form and I opted for audio. Dr Graham controlled it by touching the glass surface and I was told that I could stop it at any time to clarify something by raising a hand. It was very official, and it went on and on, and the whole time I looked at the changing colours within the glass as a point of focus as I was aware that they were all looking at me.

I didn't feel the need to interrupt the voice, though I expressed a few facial expressions of astonishment and comprehension from time to time...

I'd be living two separate lives, primary and secondary. 'Primary' would be my secret work life...where I would be 'on call' for 24 hours a day, EVERY day for special attachment duties...for the rest of my life! But it added that they probably would only need to engage me 3 or 4 times on a special attachment during my ENTIRE lifetime. The rest of the time would be assisting in research and investigation...and that would be quite infrequent too! So my main life, secondary according to them, really would be mine to do as I pleased, though with the caveat that I may be required at the drop of a hat.

The big stipulation, and it was big because of the consequences, was that I could not tell anyone ANYTHING about my 'primary life'...NOTHING!

What I do, what I see, what I hear...ABSOLUTELY NOTHING! My primary life does not EXIST in my secondary life! And the consequences if I did break the secret? Well, I would be 'removed from secondary circulation!'...Which did sound rather serious to say the least!

When the voice had finished I looked up and 'found' Dr Graham's face, "So, when I'm engaged on these special attachments as you call it, how long do they last?"

"That's down to you!" Came a quick stern voice...and my focus switched to one of the general's.

"It depends how quickly you achieve the task," he added. His face hadn't changed expression from the moment he came in. A serious military look of authority, with unblinking eyes that were penetrating my skull!

I switched my attention straight back to Dr Graham who started to speak, "It DOES depend on you, Jamie. We estimate perhaps 30 minutes of our time?..." and he looked at the other two doctors, "...but it may be shorter...it may be a LOT shorter, we just don't know for sure."

This was the first instance that I had sensed clear uncertainty. So whatever they expected me to do had not been done before.

"...and anyway, how do you know I can do it? You've not seen me do anything or had any first-hand experience with me...so how do you know I can fulfil what you want me to do?"

Dr Graham's lips twitched into a slight smile as he paused to answer...

"Let's just say that we know, Jamie…we have no doubts about you."

I'm not sure whether it was because I was on the brink of signing my life away but I started to feel a bit panicky and suddenly I was full of questions…

"So, do I have to travel far? I mean, do I go abroad for this task?"

"You don't go anywhere. You remain here, but in a different part of the complex…and you'll be under total medical supervision at all times during the attachment, so there's nothing to worry about."

"So it's not dangerous, like I can't be hurt…or killed or anything?" I continued.

"No," said the same general, "you're not going into battle!"

"No, you're not," said Dr Graham interjecting quickly, "and I'm afraid we cannot tell you any more than that at the moment until…"

"…until I commit! Yeah I know, I know" I interrupted swiftly.

There was a knowing silence as I slowly looked at each face in turn.

They needed ME so that they could achieve something; I'd known that for a while. It was some kind of secret undercover work I guess, that involved what I can do with my mind.

"And the payment?" …I continued… "You've mentioned it, but nothing has been clarified."

"Your reward…" started Dr Graham, "as I indicated to you, will be a huge amount of money for a lifetime use, it really is that much, and it would be richly deserved too. I know it all sounds cloak and dagger stuff…but I can assure you it will be life changing for you and for everyone when you complete the task. I really think it was your father's wish that you come on board with us. I just wish he was here to see you commit to us like he did. He would be so proud."

I just wish he was here as well. If I ever needed him…it was now!

I closed my eyes and saw the opening and I was through…

Meaningful City

'Ding dong ding dong…' my track of thought was interrupted by the musical sounds of my front doorbell. I glanced at my watch. It had just gone 9.30 a.m. I put the cereal bowl down on the kitchen top and walked towards the door.

"Who the heck could this be?" I said out loud.

I kicked my plimsolls, which were lying in the hallway, to one side as I unlocked the door and pulled it open.

A tall, rather pale looking chap was standing there.

He looked vaguely familiar as he began to speak…

"He knew you'd done it anyway…"

"I'm sorry?" I was completely perplexed. "What…what are you going on about?"

The man turned and started to walk away.

I moved forward and leant out of the door…

"Excuse me, excuse me…what are you going on about, who are you?" I was raising my voice but was quite calm. I was just taken aback by the oddness.

The man stopped and glanced back.

We made eye contact for a second…

("Tell him I'm missing him…tell him that for me please.")

...he raised his hand in acknowledgement of my request as he continued walking away.

I opened my eyes. It was just a blink.

No more than a second had passed.

Oh my goodness, I could jaunt at will. Talk about leaving it literally to the last second! Or is this how it's all meant to be?

"Where do you want me to sign then?" I said with a smile looking at Dr Graham. I felt such a strong link with my father. It just seemed so right.

I signed with a glass tube type pen directly onto the table top in two places and saw my signatures appearing beneath the surface. Then the doctors signed to witness the procedure and they shook my hand quite vigorously.

"Let me now show you around the base," said the other General whose name I had already forgotten.

"It's good to have you with us," he went on as he walked towards the door with Dr Graham indicating to me that I should follow.

The door duly whisked open and we walked further down the brightly lit corridor and away from where I'd been 'staying.' We turned a corner to be met by another corridor slightly less illuminated, that looked like it went on for miles! That is an exaggeration of course, but I couldn't see the end, and in the middle nearest to us were a centrally placed back to back array of connected white bucket seats.

I was beckoned to sit down by the General as everybody else in my entourage did the same, including Anna and a tall blonde lady who had joined us. I gave her a wave and she smiled back, then I suddenly felt my seat begin to rise up off the ground slightly, and we started to move silently along the corridor like a train. "I thought we were going to be attending a lecture there for a moment," I said jokingly to Dr Keifer who was sitting on my right. She gave me an agreeing polite smile as the 'train' seemed to reach its maximum speed, which wasn't fast…but fast enough sitting sideways like that. Every now and then a corridor would go by. It was like being on the London Underground with lights on the walls passing us by…but definitely not as noisy!

"My goodness! How big is this place?" I exclaimed to Dr Keifer. "I know…don't worry, you'll get used to it." she said as she smiled back again.

The little train started to slow down and as I leaned back and looked to the front area I could see the end of the tunnel coming up. It literally was like we were arriving at a brand new, very white and clean, indoor train station platform…and there were two people standing there. Dr Keifer leaned into me slightly and said, "They're waiting for you!"

I pulled an awkward face and then looked at the smiling men standing in front of me in their crisp white bodysuits, as the train came to a stop and then slowly lowered itself down like it was on a cushion of air.

"Welcome Jamie," said the taller man as he leaned towards me to shake my hand and almost pulled me out of my seat.

"My name is Dr Bradshaw, and this is my associate Dr Maskell…please follow me…"

Dr Maskell shook my hand and we walked behind Dr Bradshaw towards a huge grey metallic door, the shape and size of which resembled the big door at the white house. There were panels of lights of different shapes and colours on either side, and as Dr Bradshaw walked towards them, Dr Maskell looked at me and said, "Wait here please." I stopped and so did everyone else behind me as he went over and joined Dr Bradshaw.

I glanced back. Everybody was standing in more or less a semi-circle behind me, all looking alert and focused. I looked at Anna; her line of vision intercepted mine for an instant, but then immediately realigned past me as one of the doctor's spoke…and I turned back.

"Well…this is a particularly exciting moment for me, Dr Maskell, and everybody else involved in this project, and we would like to welcome you Jamie, and thank you for joining us."

He then put his hand up to the wall as if touching the various coloured shapes and the huge metallic door opened quite swiftly from the middle outwards. I was standing centrally to the doorway and watched the two doctors' walk into a brightly lit white tunnel, and I could see a similar large metallic door at the other end. Dr Keifer pushed on my elbow to indicate that I should follow them in and everyone else followed afterwards, and I was aware that the door closed behind us rather swiftly as soon as we had all moved inside. The walls seem to be made of an illuminated white material that curved from one side to the other forming the long dome-like tunnel. Within the glowing whiteness was a multitude of very faint thin pink coloured bands that arced across creating a very strange lighting effect as we walked the 100 yards or so on a soft grey sponge-like flooring to the other end.

Dr Maskell signified that he wanted me to stand back again, as the two doctors's stood to one side of this door too.

The school party again duly waited behind me as Dr Bradshaw began to speak...

"What you are about to see Jamie, is where we've been working for the last 25 years."

He turned towards the coloured light shapes on the wall to the right of the door, then with added afterthought, turned back again to look at me, smiled, and said with affection in his voice, "We call this...Time City." Then he swivelled back around as the door opened from the centre outwards and he and Dr Maskell walked through. He turned and beckoned me to follow and I was immediately in awe of what lay before me. We seemed to be on a huge platform overlooking a gigantic arena. My eyes were scanning from left to right as my mind tried to grasp what I was seeing. It was incredible.

"Come on, come on, come right through..." he said as he waved his hand, urging me to get closer to him. I was walking slowly and staring all the time. The sight I was seeing was mind blowing. It must be comparable to how a professional footballer feels when he or she walks out through the tunnel and into the stadium...only 10 times more overwhelming.

I was very aware of a humming sound as soon as the doors had pulled back. It was an airy, white noise that seemed to feel my head. It wasn't loud, but it was constant. There was a white dome type shape that seemed to take centre stage, probably about 500 feet across by 50 feet tall, though it was difficult to judge from this distance. In front of it and to the sides and seemingly all around it, were smaller white versions of the dome that sat in rows and I could see the 'moving' seat trains positioned here and there.

As I looked to the ends of the stadium I could see white sides banking up creating the stadium 'look' but they went ridiculously high. It was like looking at a city, but I could see no people, and I could see no roof. It just looked black. The white sided 'walls' went up and up and then just seemed to end. The black had no form or shape that I could make out, but it must be the roof.

"I cannot believe what I am seeing…it's amazing." I exclaimed.

"It is impressive when you first see it," said Dr Maskell, "but you get used to it when you've been here a while."

The big door closed behind us and as I stood there, taking in the incredible sight that lay before me, I suddenly realised that the whole grey flooring platform that we were standing on, was moving and going down. There was no noise and the movement was barely perceptible. Dr Maskell looked at me and smiled at my startled reaction as it suddenly gathered momentum and within seconds, had smoothly and calmly touched down at 'street' level below. It was extraordinary as the 'platform' just seemed to blend together with the existing grey flooring. I could see no join or break, and as I looked around I realised that the whole place was white and grey. There were no colours to be seen, although I was aware that the small white domes appeared to have those faint pink stripes running through them as well. I could definitely see it in the one directly in front of us.

"This is incredible," I said as I turned to look at the faces behind me, "are there people here? Are they all in these domes?"

Dr Keifer gestured that I should turn back around as Dr Maskell spoke, "Well…It's funny you should say that…"

"OH MY GOODNESS!" I said out loud.

Suddenly all the smaller white domes had become transparent. Their white 'shells' were no more and I was faced with hundreds of people looking my way. The white on the 'banking' had disappeared too, and again I could see loads of moving figures, which I took to be people, on different levels. The huge white dome in the middle looked even more prestigious now as it stood out like a beacon. But the sight of all these people was jaw dropping.

"I'm lost for words. I mean…it's absolutely amazing. How…how did that happen and who are these people?" I was really taken aback. I'd never seen anything like this…ever! But on saying that, there was a strange familiarity in my mind that I couldn't understand…

"They all work here, and they all knew you were coming…" said Dr Bradshaw smiling.

"Yeah, you are the promised deliverer," added Dr Maskell laughing, and he continued, "but seriously, you ARE the piece of the jigsaw that they have all been waiting for…that WE have all been waiting for…"

I didn't know how to react or what to say.

"Jamie…don't worry," added a reassuring, calm, hushed voice from behind me as I turned around. It was Anna.

"Everybody is just excited that you're here, that's all," she quietly said as she pointed at Bradshaw and Maskell with her eyebrows. I smiled. They both certainly were very eager.

"Anna! Marcie!" said Dr Graham in a tone that they understood and they reacted accordingly.

"Jamie, we'll leave you with Dr Bradshaw and Dr Maskell."

I turned to see him, Dr Keifer and Dr Michaels, Anna and new girl Marcie, walking away from me to my left. And suddenly all the domes and the banking were white and 'solid' again, and the faces were no more. I looked towards Dr Bradshaw. "Right, let's show you to your quarters…if you'd like to follow me," he said as he started walking away.

I began to follow and turned to Dr Maskell who saw my slightly puzzled expression. "It's somewhere where you can relax, have a drink, eat, use the bathroom…it's your place," he said. I nodded my head but I felt really quite overwhelmed with it all.

We walked for about two minutes or so in a straight line between the domes and I realised that the Generals were not with us anymore when I looked back. I didn't see them go, and they certainly never said goodbye.

As I was walking I touched and rubbed my hand along one of the domes. It had a solid, very smooth metallic feel and was slightly warm. "Can they still see us?" I said out loud. "Oh no, no, no," replied Dr Maskell quickly, "Wall Vision is off…they're all back to working hard," and he smiled.

"Here we are," said Dr Bradshaw pointing to a dome that we were approaching. "If you'd like to follow me around the side…"

I noticed that the domes were not completely spherical. When you were close to them you could see the shape slightly flattened towards the back and when we walked around I could see why. Dr Bradshaw put his hand up to a light pink coloured triangle shape and a door opened and he walked inside. "Come through Jamie."

I walked in, accompanied by Dr Maskell, and as soon as the door closed behind us it was noticeable how quiet it was as I could not hear the hum anymore. The lighting was so natural yet I could not see the source, and it was another jaw dropping experience, only this time it was with all the appliances and fittings. It was out of this world stuff, really futuristic. The most incredible thing from my point of view, was the screen for film and TV viewing which was basically, the wall. The viewing size could be the whole wall, or you could reduce it to whatever size you wanted…amazing! I was thinking about getting a bigger TV at home sometime, but I'd never seen anything like this. And everything was mainly white again. No colour, just greys, blacks and whites.

"What d'you think?" asked Dr Maskel as he held his hands out and looked around. He could tell by my face what I thought. "It's incredible," I replied.

"There's a bathroom through that door on the left and we've stored your clothing in the sleep room on the right there, but you'll need to wear the 'Grey' at all times when you're outside of your quarters in the city or in the hub," said Dr Bradshaw as he pointed to my latest attire.

"Clothing?…what, my actual clothing?" I questioned.

"Of course…we've brought it over, along with a few of your belongings that will make you feel more at home. It's all in your sleep room…go and take a quick look if you like. You can sort it all out when you get back from the hub."

I walked towards the door on the right and the door swished open and I walked through. Again it was natural light, and I saw the interior change instantly in a split second from dark to light as the door pulled back. There was a huge bed with glass looking units on either side and as I looked to the right I started to smile when I saw a photograph of my mother and father sitting on a 4 foot high container. I walked over and picked up the frame and looked at my parents' faces smiling back at me. "There are a few things in there too to remind you of home," said Dr Maskell standing behind me pointing at the crate. "But, come on…leave it for now, we'd better get going."

I put the photo frame back down and thoughtfully walked back through.

"Let's make our way over…" said Dr Bradshaw, "Oh, and when you want to enter and exit your quarters just present your tag to the pink triangle," he said pointing, "the green triangle is for optional Wall Vision after 6 p.m…We'll micro your hand soon though…it makes life easier…and that's your CC," he continued as he drew attention to a grey shiny panel to one side of the door.

He then raised his hand to the pink shape on the wall, the door opened, and he walked through.

Dr Maskell looked at me and nodded his head towards Dr Bradshaw, "He likes to walk everywhere, but we'll use the conveyor to the hub," and he gestured for me to follow through.

I was going along with it all, as I normally do, but It would be nice if they didn't presume I understood all the terminology.

When we got outside there was one of those chair trains sitting there waiting for us, and Dr Bradshaw had already taken a seat.

"I thought we'd take the conveyor this time," he said.

"That's fine with me," retorted Dr Maskell as he looked at me and smiled.

We were soon at the big dome, which is what they referred to as the hub. It looked just the same as the smaller domes…only a lot bigger, and I was still quite taken aback with the 'conveyor' as they called it. It just glided along with no sound and when it stopped and lowered down it looked absolutely flush with the grey spongy flooring.

"Here we are then, Jamie," said Dr Bradshaw as he got up off his seat. "This is the hub! This is what it's all about…"

Both he and Dr Maskell were so enthusiastic, it was difficult not to be swept along with it all, though at the moment I was starting to feel a little nervous.

He walked up to the panel and I watched him put his hand on the various coloured shapes, then he turned back and looked at me… "Are you ready?"

I breathed in, smiled, and nodded my head, then he turned back around and offered his hand to the pink triangle.

A huge door immediately opened up and he gestured for me to walk through into the darkened environment. It was similar to walking into a theatre just before the show was about to start, which I guess was rather apt. The light level was very comfortable, but like 'my quarters', it was difficult to determine where the source actually emanated from. The place was amazing. It was like a huge auditorium and right in the middle was a large glistening clear sphere-like bubble, probably about 30 feet in diameter, which I could tell was set below ground level. The surface was shimmering bright and sparkling like it had water running over it and I could see faint colours of green and red reflecting every now and then. It reminded me of the bubbles that you would blow as a child…only this one was a bit on the big size. It seemed to be flexing and twisting and almost spinning…it was an incredible sight. Surrounding the bubble were two big concentric circles of glass looking work stations that banked away creating the auditorium effect. In front of us there was a walkway that bisected the circles leading down to the bubble.

There were people standing here and there in front of the glass units. Some were wearing the white bodysuits like the doctors, and some were in blue. Most of them looked over at me as I stood there trying to remain calm.

The door behind had closed and I was suddenly aware that the hum sound had stopped again. The only sound was a strange swishing noise that I could tell was originating from the bubble.

"Come on, I'll take you through," said Dr Bradshaw eagerly as he pointed down the walkway. And I say 'down,' it was just a slight slope really, but I could see that the bubble was centre stage.

As we walked, I glanced left and right at the one piece glass type work stations. Their shape was scooped from the front edge backwards to the top. Just one piece; no join. A curved table and screen in one with coloured lights and shapes moving through it, very similar to the flat table lights that I experienced in the 'commitment' room. I could 'feel' eyes looking across at me from left and right, as I walked.

"Here we are, Jamie," said Dr Bradshaw as he stopped about 12 feet away from the bubble and I could see now that it was sitting on some kind of metallic base that went further down into the ground. I stood to one side of him as Dr Maskell walked past us both and went up to another glass workstation that stood on its own. "Now, after you've seen inside we're off for a briefing, so save all your questions until then if you don't mind," said Dr Bradshaw looking directly at me, "and I can imagine that you've got quite a few!"

That would be an understatement. I've wanted to question everything I've encountered so far. I've held back, really because I know this is all leading up to the big moment of truth anyway, when my 'attachment,' as they call it, will finally be revealed. To be honest, everything is so ridiculously overwhelming, my mind is just trying to take it all in and digest it all.

But right now, I actually do feel quite calm and my nervousness has subsided. I don't know whether it's to do with the serene atmosphere in here or whether it's just me adapting to the new surroundings, but I do feel quite relaxed at the moment.

Dr Maskell was concentrating on the glass workstation. His fingers sliding across the surface back and forth like he'd probably done so many times before, as the colours within the material shaped and altered. The swishing sound started to slow in momentum and I could see that the bubble was losing its iridescence and was becoming more transparent. Then a doorway opened in the base right in front of me. Streaks of pure white light broke out in all directions as if it were escaping from the confinements within. Dr Bradshaw ushered me forward and I saw a big clear glass looking chair positioned in the middle of a white lit round room. It was difficult to focus on for a moment as it appeared to be flickering in the light. Then as we got closer I realised that there were lots of black coloured lines moving in all directions within the glass structure. It reminded me of tadpoles swimming haphazardly around in a jar though these were much bigger and more like shoe laces!

I glanced at Dr Bradshaw who was now standing to one side of the chair. My expression was one of puzzlement, as my mind searched for an understanding.

"Come closer Jamie," he said, and he pointed upwards. Dr Maskell was on the other side of the chair standing in front of what looked like a lectern made of glass, his hand poised. I walked forward and looked up, and as I did, I realised we were ascending into the sphere.

"This is your homing pigeon Jamie, have a seat…it's more comfortable than it looks," said Dr Bradshaw with a laugh in his voice. I sat down in the chair. He was right. I thought it would be hard like glass, but it was very soft, and it shaped itself to me as I leaned back. The black lines carried on scurrying around beneath me and on the arm rests, which was a bit disconcerting.

"Look around you," he continued, "this is where we are going to make history…by affecting history."

I sat back up and slowly turned my head. I could see dark figures standing motionless by their coloured work stations all around me and I knew that they were all focused on me. I was inside the sphere, but I could not see it, as there appeared to be no medium between me and the work stations.

"What do you think?" said Dr Maskell as he looked at me and then held his hands out as if he was testing for rain. They were both so eager for me to approve, and of course I did.

"Right," said Dr Bradshaw, "we'll take you to be briefed now, but this is where you'll be for the attachment process and both of us will be right here with you too." I think he could tell that I was feeling rather apprehensive again.

We left the hub and took the chair train again to another dome situated further towards the top end of the 'city'.

"The two generals you met earlier should be here, along with a few other dignitaries," said Dr Maskell, as we made our way over to the doorway.

He touched my arm as if to stop me walking… "Are you alright?" he asked. I was feeling nervous again and still totally overwhelmed if the truth was known, but I answered with positive tones.

We walked inside. The lighting was like my 'quarters' and I could see various people sitting around a big glass table, similar to the one in the 'commitment' room. A tall man in a dark suit walked towards me with his hand outstretched. "Good to finally meet you Jamie. I'm John Stone, senior advisor to the president. He sends his apologies for not being here himself…come through…have a seat."

My nervousness level just jumped from 7 out of 10…to 10 out of 10!

The president?

As in the president of the United States?

He showed me to a seat and I sat down. My heart was racing, and I'm sure my face was showing it too!

"This is Steve King and Pete Bushell, two of the president's closest aides," he continued, as the other two suited men came over and shook my hand. "And everyone else I think you've met," he said pointing.

I smiled and nodded my head at the two generals and Doctor's Graham, Keifer and Michaels as Dr Bradshaw and Dr Maskell took to their seats.

"Water? Orange juice?" asked Mr Stone as his hand hovered over two jugs that were to one side of me on the table. He poured me a glass of orange juice then went to a seat opposite and sat down.

"I hope you've had a good tour of the site?" he asked, and then he glanced at Dr Bradshaw who was nodding his head.

"Let me tell you what we're doing here…

…back in the 50s early 60s a secret covert department was formed in the United States government…of which your father was part of. This black budgeted department was privy to top secret investigations that were being carried out, one of which was…the managing of extra-terrestrial occurrences and their technologies."

"You mean Aliens and stuff like that?" I asked with doubt in my voice.

"Yes indeed, I do mean that," he replied… "And let me confirm with you now to remove any uncertainty from your mind…They DO exist, and your father was involved with interspecies relations."

"What? You're saying he had actual dealings with them?" I inquired as I shook my head in total disbelief.

"I know it all sounds science fiction to you, but yes he did. He was heavily involved, and in the beginning he had some controlling capacity on the day to day management of it all and with the reporting and sharing of sensitive information with our government. But as time went on, your father was instructed to restrict the amount of data that he was conveying back to the government…so much so that he realised the department was building a wall between itself and the state. This unfortunately developed further, and soon this so-called department had expanded and became self-governing. It was so powerful, because of all the secrets it held, that it became a law unto itself…even the president was excluded from its day to day agenda…and that is so to the present day."

"So, why didn't the government do something at the time?" I asked.

"Well, they did…" replied Mr Stone, and then he paused.

"…and they were about to do more…and this is why you are here."

I was lost…and my facial expression showed it.

"I know…" he continued, reacting to my demeanour, "let me expand…

Have you heard of the Groom Lake area in Nevada?"

I shook my head.

"It's a military site that was built in the 50s and your father's department was based there. The president at the time was President Eisenhower. He was a military man himself, and he got so frustrated at the secrecy being displayed by the department that at one stage he threatened to send in the army to 'open' up the place so to speak; to find out what he, as the president, should rightfully know. But it was just a threat, and it all got smoothed over. But he knew the seriousness of what was going on, and when the presidential office changed in 1960, he briefed the new president, John Kennedy, of the situation. Now, Jack did not have the military influence that President Eisenhower had but he had the tenacity to address the political imbalance. He knew that he needed to act…and THEY knew he was going to…"

Mr Stone paused and gave me a slight smile, "this is when your father decided that he needed to act too. He was actually informed and had read documents indicating that JFK needed to be 'stopped' and by whatever means possible, and it was then that he realised that what he was part of had manifested into something that thought it was more powerful than the state…and he wanted no part of it. But he left it too late. About four weeks later JFK was assassinated in Dallas, and your father was absolutely guilt ridden knowing that he may have been able to have prevented it somehow; though he knew deep down that he was probably powerless to stop it."

"Are you saying that my father was connected, albeit indirectly...to the JFK shooting?" I asked with total disbelief in my voice.

Mr Stone deliberately paused again before replying.

"The information your father gave us, without exaggeration, was world changing, IF we could substantiate it...but unfortunately we could not. We tried by various means to infiltrate the department to access incriminating facts and evidence, and again to no avail. But your father told us of YOU, and how you were developing and what you would be able to do in the future...and a plan was hatched that instigated the creation of all this," and he held his hands out and looked from side to side.

"As you grew and advanced, we grew and advanced...and now it's the coming together of 20 odd years of planning, hoping and dreaming."

He looked at the rest of the people around the table.

"I don't mean to come across as melodramatic, but it really has become for most of us a lifelong ambition...and we're almost there." he continued, as he smiled broadly looking at me, then he looked over to the right and expectantly said, "Steve..."

Steve King nodded his head. "Yep, no pressure Jamie," then he laughed a little awkwardly as he looked at his colleagues for support in his humour.

He then breathed in deliberately slowly...and exhaled...

"What you saw earlier in the hub is a device that will connect and guide your mind to a particular place in a particular time...whereupon you will surreptitiously enter the mind of the required person, attach yourself to their thoughts and influence them."

"You're sending me back in time?" I forcibly asked.

"Yes…" he took another slow intake and exhale of breath, "yes we are, well…your mind anyway. And because as far as we know we cannot change historical facts…we're going to do something to affect the future."

I glanced at the doctors. Bradshaw and Maskell in particular were brimming with excitement, their faces full of wonder and anticipation. The generals remained stern, both upright with eyes fixed on me, as if on a 'sitting parade.'

"And this required person we are referring to…

…is your father."

I looked at him. I was absolutely stunned; my facial expression was one of total shock.

"My FATHER?" I said, completely taken aback.

"Why my father? what do you want me to do?" I said quickly. I suddenly felt very defensive.

"May I?" said Pete Bushell looking at Mr King and Mr Stone, who both nodded in approval.

"Your father at one time had certain documents in his possession…documents that if they were around today would change the world we live in completely…and for the better. They would expose the black budget dark side of the government, which is keeping so much from us. We would suddenly have access to new breath-taking life-enhancing technology and amazingly new cheaper power resources; power resources that have been available for years, but that have been kept from us. These new resources would revolutionise transport, industry, home life…everything and anything that requires power. The world would be healthier, happier and stronger…and above all…living truthfully, as at the moment it certainly is not. Mr Stone mentioned the JFK assassination…the documents would show who was really behind it…and it's this Jamie that would be the catalyst. The world's governments would snowball, not just ours, into taking collective action to undermine this falsehood that unfortunately has been existing in our lives for so long."

"So what do you want me to do then? I cannot retrieve anything physical as far as I'm aware," I said.

"Well, that would be good if you could," said Dr Bradshaw smiling.

"Yes it would," laughed Mr Bushell, "but that's not the plan," he added as he looked at Mr Stone.

"No, it's definitely not the plan…no…the proposal is this," he continued. "We want you to influence your father's mind and get him to seal the said documents in an envelope. Then we want you to get him to take this to an attorney for safe keeping, with a time delay opening for a certain date in the future that we will give to you. The addressee will be the President of the United States of America."

I nodded my head as I thought, "I see…so no factual history is being changed but when the envelope is opened in the future and the documents are read…"

"Exactly!" interrupted Mr Stone.

I continued nodding my head with my facial expression being one of approval as I immediately thought of the resemblances to scenes from a film called 'Back to the Future'. One of the characters, Doc, sends a letter to his pal Marty to be opened in the distant future. This is very close to what I've always wanted to happen with my father. For him to leave a message that I would discover in later life. Unfortunately it wouldn't be me experiencing it though, it would be the President...but I would be part of it all, WITH my father.

"How do you feel?" asked Dr Bradshaw, "you'll be seeing, hearing, doing things as your young father...probably just for a day or two in your time equating to 20–30 minutes here."

I felt fine...and I said so. I was actually looking forward to doing it, and in my mind, knowing how 'fast' my jaunts are in 'real' time, I was thinking of seconds, perhaps a minute 'away' back here.

I thought back to the experiences I've had being inside someone's mind. It was scary at first, especially with no control...but I know now that I have the capacity in me to influence when I need to. It was a good feeling...a feeling of confidence. I know now that I can almost perform at will, and being aware that it was my father's mind that I was attaching to made it sound even easier. I felt really comfortable.

Incredulous Letter

Dr Maskell and I chatted as we sat on the conveyor going back to my 'quarters.' I liked him, he seemed caring and fun. The attachment was planned for two days' time, so he suggested I relax and enjoy the comforts of my dome. He pointed out another dome that was a place to have a drink and socialise if I felt up to it, though he said to bear in mind that I was the celebrity in town, so to be aware of what that entails, which made me laugh. Optional 'Wall Vision' is available after 6 p.m. which basically is when the walls become windows, and apparently that's also when 'my colleagues' are free to roam the 'city'. I know they're all in their specific work domes at the moment, but it does feel like a ghost town...or ghost city I should say, because there literally is no one around. It was early afternoon so I had a few hours yet before I experienced the people deluge.

Everyone works and lives in this huge arena. They have time off and planned holidays as in a normal job, with special security coaches that take them back and forth to Dallas city when required. They're all working on different projects, but every one of them has been apparently connected to my 'attachment' in one form or another over the years, hence the interest in me I guess.

"Get settled in and explore your living space. Some lunch will be delivered soon," said Dr Maskell as he waved his hand at the triangle and walked inside… "and that panel there," he continued as he pointed at the inside of the wall, "is your CC, your City Communicator." I stood to one side of him looking at this rectangular grey device next to the 'shapes.' "Touch it!" he said, nodding his head towards it and then looking at me with a daring smile. I pressed my forefinger against the warm surface and immediately it lit up. There were moving images of various people that I had met, along with 'buttons' that had different wordings printed upon. "If you need any of us…just press an image and we can talk with you…and remember, after 6 p.m. the city comes to life…and only a few of us know your locality, and that's to your advantage…so be wary of Wall Vision…" he said pointing to the green triangle and laughing, "It's at your discretion, but if you want to use it, keep tapping it until you get the right combination of viewing…but don't forget, it's two way vision…is that all OK?"

I was smiling. All I wanted to do was sit down and have a drink. There was so much to take in and I was feeling somewhat overwhelmed again.

"Yeah, that's fine thanks," I replied.

"Good, I'll leave you be…enjoy your lunch."

Dr Maskell walked off and my door swished shut.

Silence.

The hum was in my head all the time when I was 'out' in the city. It was so good to have it completely quiet again.

I turned and looked around. It felt good to just be on my own. I breathed in deeply and exhaled and walked into the so-called sleep room. I picked up the photograph and looked at

164

my parents' faces and thought back for a moment, then placed it on the bed and started to open up the crate.

There was clear glass looking boxes of different sizes inside which felt soft to the touch. They all contained different possessions of mine such as toiletries, books etc and at the bottom was a box which I recognised straight away. It was my 'Jamie's Stuff' container that my mother had put together. I pulled it out and placed it on the bed.

There was no hesitation this time. I wanted to open it...sorry mum.

I picked at the masking tape until I could pull it off, then folded back the cardboard lid flaps to expose what was inside. It was like instantly going back in time. I'd seen it all before when my parents had presented it to me but it was so good to relive it. There was a yellowing newspaper from when I was born, little toy cars and plastic soldiers, a few of my baby outfits, school certificates and drawings, a Dallas Cowboy cap and scarf...and...an envelope addressed to me. Now, I don't remember that from before. I began to open it knowing that it was from my mother as I recognised her distinct handwriting on the front.

'Whirrrrr Whirrrrrr.'

I looked back up and turned around. The noise came from the front door. I put the half opened envelope down on the bed and walked out of the room. I could see Anna's face on the grey panel and I went over and instinctively touched the screen. "Come on, let me in, I've brought you some lunch."

I presented my tag to the pink triangle and the door swished open and she walked in carrying a tray.

"All freshly cooked for the special guest," she said as she walked straight past me and over to the glass table. I had a big grin on my face as I followed her. "My goodness...thank you."

She placed it down and turned back to look at me. "How's it all going? Are you OK with everything?"

"Yeah," I replied, "Not too bad I suppose…it's just a bit mind blowing really."

"There is a lot to take in," she said… "I saw you in the hub!"

"Did you? Were you at one of the work stations then?"

"Yeah," she replied… "We all said you looked a bit shell-shocked," and she laughed.

I nodded my head and exhaled.

"Don't worry…just remember you're the key that unlocks the door…or perhaps I shouldn't say that…that'll probably make you feel worse…sorry," and she laughed again.

"No, it's OK…I'm fine," I replied smiling, "do you want to sit down…?" I asked, pointing to one of the soft mini armchairs. "No, no…I'll leave you with your lunch and you can have some time on your own…but thanks anyway…Oh, did you find your personables in your sleep room?"

"Yes…I was just going through them when you came." I replied.

"Was there much?" she asked as she walked towards the sleep room.

"Er yeah…there were…a few things," I replied slightly disjointed as I followed her.

As soon as we both had entered the room she turned and whispered, *"there's never any monitoring in the sleep room, OK?…"*…I looked at her slightly taken aback…then she said out loud, "Oh yeah, quite a few bits then," and she walked

166

back past me giving me a quick 'look' as she did. I followed in her footsteps once again. "Enjoy your lunch," she said, smiling at me. "Might see you later on; or if not…I'll see you in the morning."

She looked back at me, "…and enjoy your boy's toys," and she pointed at the device on the glass table that operated the wall TV. I smiled, "Thanks Anna…"

She exited the dome and the door swished shut.

My mind was a little confused to say the least. I was trying to interpret the sleep room comment. Was she being a bit suggestive or was she simply pointing out that it was a 'private' place? And did she mean that I was being watched everywhere else in my dome? I didn't go much on that idea, but I guess that's what she was saying.

I looked at my lunch sitting there on the table. It was a burger in a bun and chips…or French fries to be exact. I picked up the tray and walked back into the sleep room and sat down on the edge of the bed. I took a big bite of the bun and then carried on opening the envelope. I pulled out the lined note paper and began to read…

Dear Jamie,

As you're reading this I think it's fair to say that I am no longer alive. And I hope you are still in your 20s and have not stored your box away for too long.

There are a few things I want to say to you and I'm sorry that you have to read it rather than hear it from me.

I am your stepmother.

I was always your mother and I loved you as such, but your father had a relationship before we met and it is she who is your true birth mother.

Please do not think any less of me for never telling you, as I wanted to every day. But your father insisted we stay solid as a family and carry on as we were. When he died I had it in my mind to inform you, but I just could not do it. I felt I was somehow being prevented from doing so. This will sound very strange, but true.

You have just left for your drive back down south as I write this, and I was going to tell you today, but something blocked me mentally. It is so frustrating.

I must also tell you to be careful for the future.

Your father loved you dearly, but he had a separate life away from us. A life that you and I were never allowed to be part of. He said that he was protecting us from complicated work issues and I never delved any deeper. But these issues did sometimes interfere in our lives, and please be aware Jamie, that they will continue to do so, even after his passing as I'm sure they involve you somehow.

Use your abilities wisely and for the good.

Love you lots and forever,

Mum
xxx

If I looked shell shocked in the hub, goodness knows what I was looking like now!

I read it through again, and I could feel my eyes welling up…

I'd always hoped I'd find a note from my father after he died; I never expected one from my mother!

I pushed the burger to one side, lay back on the bed, and closed my eyes.

I needed to jaunt.

I saw the black…then the opening…and went through.

I was looking for my mother…my earliest memory…searching. I want to go back and see. See her face.

Jane is my mother…I have no other…

I could see the blank television screen in the semi lit room and I could feel my father's comforting arms around me.

I knew it would be this.

I was sitting on his lap, 'listening' to the American pop chart 'run down' on the radio whilst my mother cooked tea in the kitchen. I felt completely at ease and relaxed…and sleepy. "I've made you some milk?" my mother announced as she suddenly appeared standing in front of us. I felt my father twitch beneath me as he awoke to her voice. I took the warm bottle from her outstretched hand and then looked into her caring eyes…"Come on, drink it all up, there's a good boy…" she said with a smile.

This is my family. This is how it has always been…

I opened my eyes.

For a moment I wondered where I was, then I turned and focused on the remains of my lunch sitting on the other side of the bed, and my mind clicked into gear. I picked up the letter again and read parts of it once more. Oh my goodness, what a time to find all this out.

I sat up and looked around my new environment. Had I been asleep as well? I walked into the main room and looked at the panel. 7.10 p.m.! I HAD been asleep.

I raised my hand to the green triangle and the window to the 'world' opened up. There were people! I immediately felt quite panicky and presented my hand to the triangle again.

One section of the wall went normal and another became clear. I waved my hand again. There was obviously a knack to get to the 'display' you required, but I did, and I arranged it such that I had one small section that was my window and I made the ceiling throughout the dome a sea of night time stars. It was quite incredible, and it really did look like the actual sky that I was looking at and not some kind of ceiling projection. It was truly an amazing spectacle. I went back into the bedroom and looked up. Yes, the ceiling had 'opened' all over the dome. I'll be sleeping under the moon tonight.

I went back over to the window section and looked at what was going on outside. There were groups of people walking by all dressed the same as me except for the colour of their body suits which were a dark blue like Anna's, and they were all filing past heading in one direction away from my dome.

I looked as far as I could see ahead of them, but I could not determine their destination. It was probably the 'social dome' that was mentioned earlier to me. I was looking but keeping back from the 'window' so as not to be seen. I was in two minds whether to venture out and follow the herd or stay in. The thought was there for a moment until the 'whirring' sound of the panel caught my attention. I went over and could see that it was Anna. I touched the screen… "Would you like an evening meal? I could bring one over if you didn't want to go out?"

That sounded superb and I agreed straight away. The 'outside world' looked a bit daunting at the moment.

She soon arrived with a chicken roast dinner which I was very grateful for, and she took great pride in showing me 'my' wine selection that lay hidden beneath the glass 'coffee' table. She pressed a 'button' on the side, and the table lifted to expose many bottles. It was movie star stuff complete with lights and dry ice.

We spent the evening chatting and I showed her the letter from my mother. She nodded her head as she read and then she looked at me…

"Remember, you are definitely the son of Arthur…he is your true father."

I pondered for a moment at her rather strange statement and then I asked… "So who is my birth mother? Do you know?"

I don't know why I asked. Why should Anna know who my birth mother is?

She hesitated then replied, "No, we're not sure who your true mother is I'm afraid."

I felt quite odd hearing her say that and I tried my best not to show it. It was just the way she said it. It made me feel like I REALLY was just a specimen in an experiment that everyone had been studying. I was probably exaggerating my feelings but just for a moment I felt a bit out on my own.

She spoke about herself more and I found out that she was a Dallas girl born and bred and said that she and her Aunt were both at Dealey Plaza at the time of President Kennedy's assassination. I had to be honest with her and confess that I didn't know much about the incident. I heard about it when I was growing up, but I had no in-depth knowledge. That did take her by surprise and I became very aware during our conversation that the 1963 event was very significant to her. She was quite taken aback regarding my lack of understanding concerning the Kennedy shooting and kept telling me to not forget my American heritage. I felt almost embarrassed for not sharing her passion and interest, especially now that I knew of my father's involvement with it all. I did remind her that I spent almost all of my life so far in England and that I was educated the English way, hence my deficiency in American history. She said that I didn't have to explain anything as she knew all about me and that really she was just teasing. The 'knew all about me' part I quite well believed but the teasing bit, no. I knew deep down that she wasn't, and some of the things she mentioned made me feel two ways in my mind. I felt like a celebrity, which I guess I did like to a certain extent, but on the other hand I was this person that was being studied and observed.

Notable Doubts

The next morning I awoke to the sounds of summer. I could hear birds twittering and the distant cooing of a wood pigeon. I propped myself up in bed. The wall opposite had turned into a huge window looking out over miles of countryside. I could see rolling fields, hedges and trees going down into a valley and up the other side…it was MY valley! Well, it certainly looked like it, though the white house was missing. It did make me look twice. I could even smell the freshness of the dew covered grass and feel the warmth of the early morning sun on my face. It was so real. It was ridiculously real. I swung my legs out of the bed and onto the floor…

…and it disappeared.

I stared at the wall…and it was just a wall once more.

I walked out into the living area and looked at the CC panel. It was 7.32 a.m.

As I turned to walk back, the panel display changed…it was Anna. I was conscious that I was in my underpants… "Good morning Jamie, I hope you slept well…I'm just about to bring your breakfast over, is that OK?"

"Err Morning…yes, that's fine…and thank you." I replied.

"See you soon," she added…with a cheeky smile.

Within five minutes my doorbell whirring thing went off and she had arrived. I greeted her in T-shirt and jeans. She walked in looking the same as she looked last night…and that wasn't a complaint…

"There you go, we thought we'd treat you to an English fry-up," she said as she placed the rather large tray on the glass 'coffee' table. It had orange juice, tea, and toast too. "Wow, thank you."

I was really hungry.

"You're more than welcome," she said with a big smile. "Your attachment is tomorrow so today we'll be going over likely scenarios and we'll be briefing you on what we require you to do. It'll be a busy time, but relaxed…although you will be meeting someone rather special. I'll call back around 8.15 for an 8.30 start. Enjoy your breakfast."

"Someone special? Who?" I asked quickly as Anna turned to leave. She looked back with a wry smile on her face then she continued on her way.

When she was 'working' she came over as very official, almost to the point of being blinkered to anything else that was going on, like she was transfixed. I've seen it a few times now. I'm not criticising her, far from it. She has a job to do. But it does make me think whether the attention she gives me is purely because of the job or whether she does really have a liking for me. Some of the things she said last night did make me doubt her true motives, but I cannot help it, I am attracted to her.

The fry-up was perfect, everything just as I like it.

I had a shower and got ready.

The grey tunic bodysuit amazed me. Apparently, it was self-cleaning and maintenance free but it astonished me how it went on and came off. When I pulled at the cuffs last night to remove it to go to bed, it somehow released its fit on me and it was so easy to take off. Putting it back on was a weird sensation as it seemed to secure itself to my body…incredible but very odd.

'Whirrrrr Whirrrr Whirrrr'

She was so punctual. It was Anna at the 'door.' The panel read 8.15 a.m.

We walked to the conveyor and sat down and I was immediately aware of the outside hum again.

"Are you looking forward to today?" she enquired as my seat began to lift beneath me and we started to move. I was a bit apprehensive but I didn't want it to show…

"I most certainly am," I replied as I looked at the people on the conveyor and those that were walking around. I felt like I'd been released from prison, venturing out, and mixing with the population. The difference here though was that they were all smiling at me, they most certainly were not wary. "Hey, morning!"…"How's it going?"…"Good morning!" People were calling out with the occasional wave…I REALLY feel like a celebrity. Mind you, I stood out like a sore thumb in my grey bodysuit with everybody else in dark blue!

I felt really good as we arrived at the destination dome, which was right over the other side of Time City behind the hub. Anna took me inside and I was greeted by Dr Maskell.

"Good morning to you! Big day tomorrow Jamie…come on through, how are you feeling?"

We chatted as he took me along a corridor and then into a room with rather comfortable looking seating that was all facing the same way like a cinema. Dr Bradshaw walked towards me.

"Morning Jamie…" He ushered me to an awaiting small sofa which was a replica of the one in my dome.

"We're going to be showing you a few probable scenarios of what you are likely to encounter on your attachment. What you will see is not real. It is a virtual display of what we envisage will take place due to information provided to us by your father."

To hear my father mentioned again still came over as unfamiliar, but it was a good feeling at the same time.

I sat and watched three likely experiences that I may have. They were all very similar with very slight variations, and they were SO real. Dr Bradshaw and Dr Maskell stopped the 'act' at certain points to suggest what I should be 'doing' or should I say what I should be 'willing' my father to do. It was a very strange few hours, sitting there watching my father go about his day to day business. He was young, energetic, in control…and alive. But I was assured again when I expressed my amazement at the lifelike quality of what I was viewing, that it was simply just a programmer's technical excellence in reproducing my father's recollections.

We stopped for coffee mid-morning which was brought in by the delightful Anna. She smiled at me and I knew that was all I could expect, though she did point at the digestive biscuits with a knowing expression on her face.

After lunch I was introduced to many people who were directly involved with the hub and the Time City development. Their enthusiasm for the 'project' and their overwhelming desire for me to complete the attachment was incredible. I know that Dr Bradshaw had said sometime earlier that I was the final piece of the jigsaw so to speak, making me sound like some kind of saviour. But speaking with these people really made me perceive how important I was to them, and how much they were relying on me. The seriousness of it all started to kick in. I'd always known this wasn't a game, but the fun side of me had made light of it all, and now the magnitude of the whole situation and the realisation of what it all meant to everybody involved was starting to sink into my carefree, easy-going mind.

And then I was introduced to the 'special person.'

There was a bit of scurrying around and anxious looks on the doctor's faces before she came in and I realised that someone important was expected.

It was Jackie Kennedy, the wife of President John Kennedy who was assassinated in 1963. She was a lovely lady, full of charm and femininity and I had to apologise to her for not having the proper full knowledge and understanding of what took place. I felt embarrassed again like I did with Anna, and I explained that I am an American but as I lived near enough all my life in England and was raised the English way, American history and politics were not part of my curriculum. It was a repeat performance of my excuses to Anna, and she said that she understood, though I think she was just being nice. We must have talked for a good 30 minutes or so, after which I could totally appreciate and understand her passionate interest and involvement in what was going on in Time City.

She wanted and needed to know why her husband was killed and she wanted and needed to know who was truly responsible. Her sadness remained strong after all these years and her strive for justice was stronger than ever. I could feel the ingrained anguish in her voice as she described the frustration of still never being able to believe the obvious conclusions after all this time.

She said I was going to "open the gate to the pathway of truth."

My goodness, she made me emotional.

I couldn't help it. I felt empowered.

I was back in my home dome around 5.00 p.m. The afternoon had been quite a draining experience and to be honest it had mentally tired me out. I could almost feel my brain aching. The Jackie Kennedy visit really stuck in my mind and I found out after, through Dr Bradshaw, that a majority of the funding for everything going on in Time City was actually being provided by her!

I lay on my bed and thought back to what she had said and then to what the 'president's men' had said. She was obviously trying to get to the bottom of her husband's assassination whereas the president's aides were more concerned with this so-called secret government and the alien connection…and the two were connected, unbelievably, with my father.

I was still looking forward to the attachment, although the pressure of making sure I carried out everything correctly was 'playing on my mind'. Dr Maskell had said, when he escorted me back, to try and relax and not let the red tape side of it all get to me. But that was easier said than done.

I started to read my mother's letter again. I was still trying to get my head around that too.

I placed it back in the box, and as I did I noticed another smaller brown envelope tucked down the side. It was a plain brown envelope with some words written upon it…

'This may be useful'

It was my father's spidery writing!

I stared at it for a moment.

I couldn't understand how I missed it when I went through the box, though I know I stopped 'looking' when I came across my mother's letter. It was a bit camouflaged I guess AND it was almost stuck to the side of the container too.

I couldn't believe it!

First my mother, and now finally my father!

At last! I could feel my mind buzzing with excitement. This is what I'd always longed for.

What revelation is he going to tell me?

The envelope looked really old and parts of the gummed back had lifted and were not attached. I opened it and pulled out...a business card.

'Meaji Merill Associates'

I kept looking at the card.

It didn't mean anything to me at all. I started to search my mind looking for any clues.

I kept looking at it...my mind wandering back...

I closed my eyes and looked for the black...then the opening...and went through...

...the man walked over.

"We are deeply shocked at your loss, Jamie. To lose your father and now your mother...it creates such sadness."

"Thank you..." I responded as I slowly nodded my head. I could feel the awkwardness in my thoughts as to the correct reply...

"We're going to a local hotel afterwards for some tea and sandwiches if you can make it?" I said as I cocked my head to one side looking at the woman standing behind him.

"That is kind of you, but we have to go back now," he replied, and then he held out a business card... "Please...contact us if you feel the need."

I took it from him and glanced at the printing.

'Meaji Merill Associates'...I saw the words...

"Thank you," I replied as I immediately pushed the card into my trouser pocket, and I could feel the slight puzzlement in my thoughts...

I opened my eyes...

...and looked at the card that was still in my hand.

How on earth did that get in my keepsake box?

It couldn't have happened. I don't remember what I did with it afterwards, but I certainly didn't open the box and put it in. My father must have had another business card. That was the simple explanation. But it certainly had me thinking.

I looked closely and turned it over and examined the back. It had no telephone number or address. It was just plain black, no writing, no picture...and then as I was about to look away I saw a face.

I looked back.

It was just a soft faint grey outline on the black card that seemed to fade almost immediately, but I saw it. It was a woman's face.

I kept looking.

Nothing.

Did I imagine it?

Perhaps I saw what I wanted to see. Was it my mother?

It may have been.

I kept looking...

Nothing.

I looked at my father's writing on the envelope again.

'*This may be useful*'

My frustration was growing as I put the card back in the envelope and then back in the box. To say I was disappointed was an understatement.

I got up and walked out into the living area and looked over at the panel. I wanted to see Anna. I hesitated as I looked at the time. It read 5.58 p.m. and then it suddenly changed to Anna's animated moving picture as the 'whirring' sound began. I went over and pressed the screen…

"Hello young man, would you like dinner and some company?"

She was in 'out of work' mode for sure.

"You must have read my mind," I replied.

"Give me 10 minutes and I'll be over," she said.

The screen reverted to the time display as I turned on 'wall vision.' I immediately altered it as many people were already 'walking towards me' from their work domes which made me slightly panic for a moment. That sounds ridiculous I'm sure, but I really did not want my whereabouts known to anybody else in Time City. I liked the secrecy of my stay here.

Anna was soon at my dome and she was accompanied by Dr Maskell.

"I hope you don't mind me coming along too, Jamie…though I don't want to be a thorn between two roses," he said with a laugh as he looked from side to side at me and Anna.

I almost felt myself blushing, which doesn't happen often.

Anna put the little tower of food down on the table and played host as she always did.

"How are you feeling about tomorrow then?" asked Dr Maskell as he tucked into his pasta salad.

"I'm OK really," I replied… "I just want to do it now and get it done."

"Good, good," he added as he chomped away.

"I do find it really strange though how my father is talked about as if he is still alive."

"I know…because we worked with him and in a sense WILL be working with him again through you, we tend to speak about him in the present tense. I'm sorry…"

"No, it's OK," I responded, "It's a nice feeling really."

"What was he like to work with?" I asked with a smile in my voice as I too chomped away.

Dr Maskell smiled back and hesitated as he finished off and swallowed what he had in his mouth.

"He was a brilliant man, Jamie, and he was a pleasure to be around."

"Did he have to wear one of these body suits too?" I asked with a smile as I pointed to my attire.

"Oh no," laughed Dr Maskell, "he got away with dressing as he wanted, and that was quite casual…slacks and an open neck shirt was his uniform."

That really surprised me but I never said anything.

"His enthusiasm rubbed off on everyone…wouldn't you say, Anna?"

I looked at Anna for her response as I took another mouthful.

She looked up at me, and then looked over at Dr Maskell as if digesting the question as well as the food, then looked back at me… "Yep…he always made you feel part of the team…like you were the most important person."

I was surprised again as I looked at Anna with a perplexed look on my face.

She looked back at me with her own puzzled look…

I finished off and swallowed what I was eating.

"…well, I thought you said you hadn't met him? Or am I getting confused?…"

Anna stared at me, "no…no, I had met him…very briefly though when I first started here years ago. We didn't work close…I was more in the background really…but…he still made an impression on me, although much of it was via other work colleagues who were closer to him really…"

I nodded my head as I ate some more.

'Whirrrr Whirrrr.'

I turned my head towards the wall panel.

Anna jumped up and went over. "It's Mr Stone, Jamie…shall I open it for you?"

"Err…yeah, OK, thank you."

"Hello Anna," said Mr Stone as she stood back for him to see the rest of the room.

"…and hello Doctor…I just wanted to wish you the best of luck for tomorrow, Jamie. If you could be in the hub for 8.30 a.m. please for final briefing and preparation. Enjoy the rest of your evening."

It was short and sweet, but good of him to say I guess.

I looked at Dr Maskell after the screen went back to time mode.

"Will there be a lot of people there tomorrow?"

"The key workers will be with you in the Hub…and everybody else in Time City will be watching from inside their domes."

"Everybody?" I exclaimed as I sat back.

"Yep, everybody. It's a big thing, Jamie. We've all been looking forward to tomorrow for a long time…and I don't want to sound like a party pooper, but after we've eaten I think me and Anna should go and you should get some early shut eye."

"I'll be fine, don't worry. It's not like I'm doing anything physical," I responded.

"I know, but the chair will drain you…mentally drain you. You'll feel like you've just run a marathon when you return. Honestly…it will. I know it's just directing you and guiding you and it's you that's doing the real 'work'…but it WILL tire you…so just be aware."

I nodded my head again in appreciation of what he said. But I was sure I wouldn't feel like that. I've never had any mental or physical fatigue after any jaunt before, and as far as I could see, this was just another jaunt. The only difference being, that this one had a guidance mechanism attached.

It did make me wonder how he knew that it would possibly tire me, but I just took his word.

Anna and Dr Maskell stayed for about another half hour then made their way back to wherever their home domes were situated. Anna said she'd see me tomorrow around 8.15 a.m. to escort me to the hub. So what she really meant was she'd be here AT 8.15 a.m. on the dot!

I was feeling quite excited as I lay on the bed with thoughts rushing through my mind about the attachment. I did think about the two instances of conversation regarding my father that caused me to self-analyse the situation. My father always, without fail, would wear a tie when leaving the house and especially when he went to work. I could never recall EVER seeing him going out with just an open neck shirt. I almost feel that would have stuck in my mind if he HAD of done that. Mind you, I never knew anything about his 'secret' job so perhaps basically it was this other side of him that I never got to appreciate. It makes me feel a bit sad though because I always thought that I understood all his idiosyncrasies and living mannerisms, but it seems he was living a double life.

The other instance that made me 'sit up' was with Anna. I could have sworn she had said days ago that she had not met my father, and now she was saying that she had. But does it matter whether she had or had not? It was only me making something of it. Mind you, I could tell her slight awkwardness when I questioned her…

I suddenly wished to be back in my uncomplicated normal quiet life. To be standing on the back lawn of my new house, with the sun beating down from a rich blue cloudless sky as I absorb the breath-taking panoramic rolling countryside view in front of me…which hopefully would also include the white house…if it hasn't been moved! The thought was a light hearted one but it still made me wonder again at the missing structure in the wall viewing…and I closed my eyes to imagine it for myself…

…and saw a woman's face. Her white skin so smooth and unblemished, her hair so beautiful, so golden blonde, falling gently across her dark blue eyes. She swept it back with her soft long hands as her fine lips twitched into the shape of a knowing smile. I reached out to touch her face, she was so close. Her hands clasped my hand and tenderly squeezed. I could feel her caring love…it was real, I could feel her warmth.

I know she should not be here but I am glad she is.

I must remember this…please let me remember this.

"Wake up sleepy head…quick, dad's home!"

I opened my eyes to see my mother leaving my bedroom. She turned back, "Come on Jamie, he's just coming in the front door…quick, jump to it."

I leapt out of bed and followed my mother down the stairs.

"Hello little man!"

My father had his arms out wide and I ran into his body and we hugged.

"Have you been a good boy for mum?" he asked, as his hand ruffled through my hair.

"I'm always good…aren't I mum?"

Jane laughed. "Yes, you are…most of the time."

"How's you? Is everything OK at work?" she inquired as they both kissed.

"Yes, its fine, but the Man is making it difficult, so I've been advised that they're moving us again…I'm sorry."

Jane sighed and gave Arthur a hug as I watched them both. It was almost in slow motion as my father turned to look at me…his immaculate shirt and tie looking at me too…

"Come here boy, you're not missing out on a family cuddle."

I forgot how loving he was.

We stood, grabbing hold of each other…until my mother started tickling me…

"Mummmmmmm…" I said giggling, as I pulled back; realising how close I was to the edge and then I felt a touch upon my shoulder. I turned to see her face, her compelling beautiful face. Her eyes so dark yet so full of light, transfixed onto mine as her thoughts engaged. This was her last visit and her sadness was obvious, but there was also excitement and

urgency. I could not look away…I did not want to look away. Her face filled my vision like a beacon to my gaze. We went back to the edge and she showed me the blackness as I looked down into its eternal dark depth. It was the way through. But I had to want to go. And I know SHE wanted me to go, I could feel it. But her full thoughts were being masked, I could feel that too. But I'd always known about the blackness and I'd wanted to go before. I felt confused…

I opened my eyes and erratically looked around the bedroom of my dome as if helping my mind search for answers to the mixed up feelings I was having.

I got off the bed and walked into the living area. The panel read 9.42 p.m. I went over to it and pressed it to display the contacts, then pressed Anna's moving figure. "Come on Anna," I said out loud.

The figure kept 'blinking' but there was no response. I pressed for Dr Maskell…

"Hi Jamie…is everything alright?" he replied after a couple of seconds. I could see he was still in his 'work suit.'

"Yeah, I'm fine…I was just wondering if you could come over, or if I could meet you somewhere. I just want to ask you a few things…"

"You should be settling down for the night you know, big day tomorrow," he replied.

"I know, that's what I want to talk to you about…sorry…I've just got a couple of things on my mind I want to ask you. It'll just take a few minutes…honest," and I laughed, but my laugh was a bit false.

"OK, hold on…I'll be over shortly."

"Thank you…I'm sorry."

"It's OK…see you in a while," and he switched off.

I sat down on one of the sofa chairs and exhaled.

I'm probably making a mountain out of a molehill here and I just need some reassurance, but a few things are just starting to put little doubts in my mind. I've always thought of the blond haired women as some kind of guardian angel. Was it she that was showing me, trying to confirm it for me, as if to back up what I'm thinking?

'Whirrrrrrr Whirrrrrr'

Dr Maskell was here.

I let him enter and he started talking immediately…

"Are you having reservations about tomorrow? Honestly Jamie, don't worry. We know your ability, and what you can do…you've been there and done it before…well, OK…you haven't ACTUALLY been to this other time and place, but we know your capabilities. All that we're doing is assisting you by guiding you in, and let me assure you that your health and wellbeing will be constantly monitored…although you may even complete the attachment at your end before the monitors have a chance to 'get going' at our end…" he started laughing.

I looked at him. How could I doubt anything he said? He always came across as a kind, fun loving, genuine man, and his enthusiasm to the project and to me was immense.

"I know, I know," I said as I looked down at the floor. We sat down on the mini sofas…

"So what is it, Jamie? come on…I think you know you can trust me now, tell me…what's troubling you?"

I breathed in deeply and exhaled. "I'm sorry…" I said as I looked up at him. "Don't get me wrong, I trust you…and

Anna…but sometimes, things are said, and it just, well…it just triggers thoughts in my mind…"

"Like what, Jamie…what d'you mean?" Dr Maskell asked.

"It's going to sound silly…"

"No, come on…just say it"

I looked him directly in the eyes. I liked Dr Maskell and I didn't want to give offence by suggesting I distrusted him…

"This may sound really daft and trivial, but it means something to me…it was when you mentioned that my father wore open necked shirts…"

"Did I? OK, so why is that bothering you?"

"Well…he never went casual like that. It was just one of his ways. If he ever went out or went to work…he ALWAYS wore a tie."

Dr Maskell looked at me and then let out a half laugh of disbelief.

"And this is what has made you doubt me?"

"I'm not doubting you…it just makes me re-evaluate the situation, that's all."

"And Anna?" he asked, "was it because you thought she'd said she hadn't worked with your father…and she had?"

"Yes…exactly that," I replied. "It just stuck in my head…"

"And you're sure she said that she hadn't worked with him before?" he asked.

"No, I can't say for certain…but I'm pretty sure," I replied.

Dr Maskell got up and took a few paces then looked at me.

"Jamie…if it wasn't for the fact that we have to wear these white bodysuits, I certainly wouldn't be able to tell you what I wore yesterday let alone years ago. I honestly don't remember for sure what your father wore when he worked here and I'm sorry if I've sowed the seeds of distrust by saying otherwise. I probably just said it in the conversation…I cannot tell you any more than that."

I nodded my head in an agreeable gesture.

"And as for Anna…she's been unwell for a while now, Jamie. She's got personal family issues and I'm sorry if that's come over during her time with you…"

"No, not at all…is she OK?" I alarmingly interjected.

"Yes, she's fine…we were in two minds whether to take her to one side, but it seems things have come to a head on their own and she's asked to take some leave. So…as you can probably gather, she's not been entirely focused recently in Time City."

"No, I understand, I'm sorry to hear all that. Will I see her again?"

I felt really concerned for Anna as she'd not hinted at any problems, but then again she probably wouldn't have mentioned anything to me anyway…she is too professional and committed to her job. I felt frustrated though that I had to hear it from somebody else…

"Oh yes, I'm sure she'll be back sometime…when things have sorted themselves out at home."

Every picture tells a story as they say. I just wasn't looking hard enough. It made me think how wrapped up I was getting in my own day to day life now and how unaware I had become of other people's lives.

I felt guilty and also annoyed with myself for allowing it to happen as that's not the sort of person I am or have been.

I reassured Dr Maskell before he went that I was OK, and I was. It was good talking with him. He said that Anna had already left Time City on one of the evening coaches back to Dallas. I was really surprised though that she had never 'buzzed' me to tell me that she was going. I really liked Anna and I was going to miss her. I still pressed her moving motif on the communication panel before I went to bed…just in case.

Attachment Day

I awoke the next day to the sounds of the Somerset countryside once more. I sat up and looked at the amazing view again across the valley. It amazed me how real it all seemed. I just stared for a while, exploring the scene. How is this done? I can even smell the open fields, hear the occasional sheep, feel the warmth of the sun…see the white house on the horizon! Yes, it was there…it had returned.

I felt a bit strange as I focused on the majestic structure in the distance. They've obviously got their act together this time with the visual reproduction…

I got out of bed and immediately as I stood on the floor…it was all gone.

I walked out into the living area. The time display read 7.34 a.m.

Dr Maskell said he would call around at 8.00 a.m.

I touched the screen display then pressed Anna's communication motif. I knew there would be no response…but I just had to do it again.

'Whirrrr Whirrr!' it startled me for a moment.

I touched the screen again and saw a woman's face.

"Hi Jamie, I'm Marcie…I've got some breakfast for you…"

I smiled. It was a new face, though the name rang a bell.

I opened the door.

"May I?" she asked, as she gesticulated with her two hands holding the tray to come in.

"Yes, yes…please do." I responded as I beckoned her inside.

She was a tall, long legged, slim woman in her mid-twenties, with shoulder length blond hair, blue eyes and a warm smile. "Thanks very much," I said as she placed it on the table and turned to leave.

"Best of luck today, Jamie," she said in a very strong American accent as she adjusted her body suit belt, probably more by habit than for a reason.

I smiled and thanked her. "Will you be staying in your dome tonight afterwards?" she enquired as she moved towards the doorway. "I don't actually know," I replied, slightly taken aback. I had no idea what was going to happen after the attachment. "I would guess so I suppose," I added.

"I'll be on your CC soon, so if you fancy some company, please contact me."

I smiled again, "OK…thanks," I replied, as she turned and walked out.

The door swished closed and I walked over to the table, stopped, and walked back to the display panel…and touched it. Anna's moving motif had already gone…and there was Marcie in her place!

I just stared at 'her' for a moment. Goodness me, it's one out one in…no messing around! I felt quite strange though that Anna had left in the way that she had, and without even a goodbye. Ridiculous to say it, but I almost felt hurt. Just get a grip, Jamie!

I sat down and had my breakfast at the table, freshened up in the bathroom, then got my body suit out and put it on…or should I say, it put itself on me.

8 a.m. on the dot, 'Whirrrr Whirrrr'…"Morning Jamie, all set for the big one?"

I looked at Dr Maskell; his face grinning from ear to ear as he shook my hand. Does this chap ever lose his excited enthusiasm I wonder? I was feeling a bit nervous now as we boarded the awaiting chair train.

"I met Marcie earlier…she seems nice…is Anna OK though?"

"Marcie is a lovely girl…and Anna is fine, don't worry," responded Dr Maskell smiling and laughing… "Come on, we've got to concentrate on matters in hand…we've got work to do!"

I looked at him and smiled. He was right, I needed to focus, but Anna's departure from my little world was rather odd, and it was on my mind.

I was aware again of the constant monotone humming sound in the air as the chair train rose up off the ground and silently started to move, passing Time City workers along the way who cheered and passed on their best wishes. I felt like a pop star, I really did…it was so surreal.

We stopped outside the hub and I followed Dr Maskell inside. As the door closed behind us, the humming abruptly stopped and the swishing sound of the bubble took over. All of the work stations were occupied and I was aware of excited body and head movements as we walked down the sloping soft pathway to the entrance. Dr Bradshaw was there and extended his hand to greet me.

"Morning Jamie, here we are then…the day has arrived. How do you feel?"

"I feel fine thanks, I was a bit nervous earlier, but seem OK now," I replied.

"Good. Everything is ready. All systems are go as they say…and we've got a full house too."

I looked back and up to the sea of faces who were looking 'down' at me.

"Wait until you get inside, then you'll see the full 360," added Dr Bradshaw.

"…Don't worry," said Dr Maskell as he could tell I was looking a bit perturbed by that last comment. "You'll see all the faces but only for a short period. When the bubble's time mechanism begins, WV will switch off from your point of view."

I nodded my head in appreciation at what he said as Dr Bradshaw waved his hands in different directions over the glass workstation and gradually the swishing sound over the bubble started to slow down. I was aware that the sphere was becoming transparent as the entrance door swished open. Brilliant white light streaked out in all directions as I felt Dr Maskell's hand on my back urging me to move forward. With my eyes adjusting to the inside luminance I focused on the glass looking chair sitting centre stage. I could see the many dark coloured shapes moving around inside its crystal fabric as I walked closer. This changed as I got closer and I could see the thin squiggly lines, like shoe laces, moving around haphazardly.

"Are you alright, Jamie?" asked Dr Maskell, as again he put his hand on my back. It was just a statement rather than a true question because he moved over to the chair's workstation as soon as he'd said it.

And I was alright. I felt excited but I felt confident too. I had my father in my mind now and I was looking forward to being in HIS mind!

"Is everything quite clear; the different scenarios? What you need to do?" said Dr Bradshaw.

"Yep, all systems go with me too," I casually and jokingly answered.

"Right…if you'd like to get on the chair then, Jamie…and we'll ascend into the bubble."

I sat down and swivelled to lie partially back. I could feel the soft fabric, foam like material, moulding itself slightly around parts of my body as I placed my arms onto the rests, which again gave a similar experience. I felt I could get up if I wanted too, but at the same time, I felt comfortable and secure.

"We're going up," announced Dr Maskell as I dropped my head back to look at the roof which was opening like a camera lens aperture, revealing the inside of the sphere. I could feel the soft foam type fabric 'holding' my head in place. I tried to move my head forward and did so. The fabric had immediately released its 'grip' and I let my head rest back again.

We slowly reached the required position and I looked around at the arena of faces that were focused upon me. I literally felt like a goldfish in a bowl. There must be a hundred or so people here, including, I was told, the generals and the president's aides along with the president of the United States watching at home in the white house on closed circuit television! My goodness, I raised my eyebrows in disbelief and amazement at that when Dr Bradshaw mentioned it. I did say to him that it literally might be over in a blink of an eye, so it's probably not going to be good viewing. He said that they estimated that I would be 'out' for 28 minutes. No idea how they know that...but it's still not going to be good viewing just watching me laying there!

Dr Maskell came over and leaned towards me... "You'll hear a voice in a moment introducing the event...you know what us Americans are like for a bit of theatre and razzamatazz!" And he smiled.

Sure enough, as if on cue:

"The President of the United States, Mrs John Kennedy and family, Generals, ladies and gentlemen...welcome to the hub in downtown Time City...

November 22nd 1963, is etched into our minds as a date the world changed...for the worst. We lost our president. A president that was going to open the world to new technologies...new beginnings...and new life. HIS life was cut short...and that consequently deprived our lives of what he was going to provide us with...THE TRUTH!

Today is November 22nd 1986. Today will also be etched into our minds...but this time, for a whole much better reason."

Did I hear him correctly? Did he say it's November 22nd? I know I've lost track of time since I've been here...and I don't even know which day of the week it is...but it can't be November. It's summer for goodness sake...we're in June, possibly July now...but not November!

I glanced at Dr Maskell. He was looking at me and raised his eyebrows as he nodded his head forward and mouthed,

"Are you OK?" He could obviously see the changed expression on my face.

I attempted to move my right arm to beckon him over but I couldn't. I tried my left, and then tried to push up with my body. I could not. The chair was preventing me. I looked down at the clear plastic like material that was 'gripping' me. The black wriggly shoelace lines were now straight and moved around slowly in parallel groups of 3 and I could feel the warmth from the chair on my back.

I nodded my head to Dr Maskell in a reluctantly accepting type manner. I'd been here before. My 'ward' experience was more or less like this, unable to move…and I guessed like then, this was done for a purpose. I relaxed back in the seat, though my mind was working overtime with the November issue.

"Something special and unique is going to take place today. A momentous event like no other…that will go down in history as a great happening. A great happening that will unlock other great happenings…and you are here to deservedly witness it…because without your hard work and dedication over the many years…we couldn't have come this far…so thank you…

And now…it's time to fit the final piece of the puzzle into place. I know most of you have never met this guy…but I know most of you will think that you have. You know him as 'Jimbo' …it's Jamie Miller!"

Oh my goodness, this was terrible. I felt so awkward, so exposed. They were clapping and cheering. Even Dr's Bradshaw and Maskell joined in.

I smiled. I didn't know what else to do. I didn't raise my hand to wave…because I couldn't!

What was next? Cheerleaders and band music?

Dr Maskell suddenly appeared by my side as the Time City audience disappeared from my view. "Sorry Jamie, like I say...us Americans and our theatre!"

"And what's this with the Jimbo thing?" I asked with a confused look on my face.

"It's the name they've called you over the years...just an affectionate nickname, that's all."

Then Dr Bradshaw came over to the other side of the chair. "You've been part of their lives for ages...when this is over today you will be like a king to them...if you're not one already! You'll be a world figure...a superstar. Every day in your life will be full because everybody will want to interview you, be with you...Godddd, you'll be famous!"

"Are we ready gentlemen?" came the voice from outside the bubble as Dr Bradshaw put his hand up and backed away to the glass workstation.

"Just do your normal thing, Jamie...and remember we're guiding you, but you won't be aware of anything different. Tell us when you're ready then wait for our mark before you go...and good luck!" said Dr Maskell giving a thumbs up supportive gesture.

I suddenly felt immense pressure.

Dr Bradshaw has a way with words...NOT!

I certainly DO NOT want to be THAT famous. I just want a quiet life, and the only thing I want my days to be full of...is clean country air! I'd be lying if I said I didn't like the celebrity lifestyle that I'm mildly receiving here in Time City. But it sounds like it wouldn't be a patch on the 'outside' if Dr Bradshaw's words come true.

If they're monitoring my vital signs like they say they were going to, my blood pressure must be quite high now!

"Just relax and give me the nod when you feel you're ready, Jamie."

I was suddenly aware of the swishing noise that had started again and it was getting louder as I averted my sight upwards. I then glanced over at the two doctors who had their heads down, 'operating' the work station. Dr Maskell looked up at me. He was waiting for my signal. I looked away and across to the other side. My breathing was heavy as I tried to compose my thoughts into some sort of orderly fashion. Why was I getting panicky? I've done this loads of times. Like one of the General's had said, I'm not going into battle.

It was probably just the razzmatazz of the situation and knowing that everyone in the mini world I was living in at the moment was watching…and let's not forget the President of the United States too for goodness sake!

I was gaining control and I swallowed what saliva I had left in my dry lipped mouth. I turned my head to face the doctors who were both staring at me. I engaged my line of sight with Dr Maskell's…and nodded…then turned back…and closed my eyes…

Tracking Time

The strong smell of petroleum filled my senses as we closed the door behind us and looked across the vast desert space of the airfield. We were standing in the shade but I could feel the temperature increase almost immediately as if it were MY skin registering the warmth.

I could see that the hills in the distance were shimmering and wobbling in the haze of the incredible early morning heat as we stepped out into the full force of the sun and began to walk across the expanse of concrete towards hanger five.

"Morning!" said two airmen as they walked past, quickly saluting.

My father responded, "Morning!" and nodded his head towards them.

As we got to the door he habitually checked his collar and tie, punched in the code, and went inside.

The coolness hit me and the relief was instantaneous.

"Morning Don, you're in early…did they arrange a special plane for you?"

He said it with a humorous sarcastic tone, and I liked it. It was certainly something I cannot say I've ever really experienced with him before. It was good hearing his voice too…it seemed quick and alert…and of course…young.

Don looked serious and stern as he pointed towards the office and we walked inside.

"You've seen the memo then…" he rhetorically asked as he went behind the desk and pulled open a drawer and took out a packet of cigarettes… "And have you burnt it? Or disposed of it?"

I knew that my father had read it last night and that it was in his safe.

"Yes," lied my father, "…I've got rid of it!"

Don nodded his head in approval as he fumbled with his lighter then sucked in the smoke and blew it out vigorously.

"…and I take it you're pleased then?" he went on… "This is what you wanted isn't it?"

I could feel the satisfying thoughts in my father's mind as we replied, "It needs to be done, there's no other way I'm afraid."

"There's always another way Bernie," fired back Don, "and you know it. We need to do something, I agree, but this is going too far…It's crazy!"

I could feel my father tensing, but I could also feel that his thoughts pertaining to the conversation were very relaxed. He knows what's going to happen…and he's for it!

My mind is racing. I'm totally confused. If I had a collar I would be hot under it. My father WANTS it to happen. I can feel it. There's a document in his safe that is basically seeking a vote from him to authorise the murder of the President…and he is going to agree and say YES. I know it because I know his thoughts! He is a member of some high powered group or organisation…and who is Bernie? Why did he call my father, Bernie?

We walked over to a mirror completely without any influence from me, although I was thinking to myself that I wanted to see him. And there he was, my young father, adjusting his tie, shifting it from side to side as he pushed the knot higher. It was definitely him. Just for a moment I doubted the mind I was in, but no…it most certainly was my father and the timing of my 'entrance' so to speak was spot on. Hat's off to the Time City people!

We turned to face Don.

"Crazy it may sound," said my father rather loudly, and then we walked over to the door and closed it, then looked back at Don… "Crazy it may sound," he continued in a lower voice… "But we've got to stop him properly. He's going to persist until he breaks us…I know it, and so does Allen. We can't let this upstart expose us and all we've been doing. It's not right…and you know it too!"

It just didn't sound right hearing my father talk this way, and what made it worse was that I could understand his thought patterns that were backing up the verbal. I felt very awkward and my thoughts were running amuck in my own mind.

What was I sent here to do? To uncover the organisation that is hiding the secrets that the world needs to know. To rid us of the untruths allowing the world to gain the undercover technical knowledge and knowhow, which will bring a better way of life to our planet's inhabitants. And let me not forget Mrs Kennedy and her family. She wants to know the truth too. The talk I had with her really affected me and I wanted to do this for her as well.

So with all this in mind, and it certainly was ALL in mind, I now find out that my father's views to do with all this are rather different to what I've been led to believe. He must have changed his ideas later on because he came to the government for protection so he must have done a U turn in his thoughts, but it wasn't nice to hear and appreciate his feelings at the moment. They are certainly quite scary to say the least, emanating from a man who was gentle, kind and loving…my father!

I started to think of the route to the 'future'…or should I say, to the present. If I influence my father and do what I came here to do, does that mean that he went to the government because I made him? He wants to get rid of the president. I can feel it clearly, and his thought patterns are so wrong in my mind. But is it right that his son from the future influences what he does now? I was getting quite moralistic, but at the same time I was thinking of what I knew from 'my time' and what I had learnt. I was here to make things better for a lot of people; I could improve the world in so many ways if I carried out this attachment. It was just my father creating this hesitation. Why does he think like this?

I decided to lay low and observe; listen, and try to make sense of his thought processes before I attempted any influence.

For the next few days I literally did just that, and there were instances where I received certain thoughts from him that were absolutely mind blowing.

Extra-terrestrial life forms definitely DO exist! My father is involved with them and there are plans to integrate them into our society as an existence with the long term plan of evolving alongside them in the distant future. I could feel my father's passion and the strong link he had with these alien beings. He had many dealings with them over the years;

communication was frequent and agreements had taken place. It was impossible though for me to actually delve deeper to obtain more information. There was a barrier in his mind that I could not cross. I could feel the resistance to my ability. It was a blockage that had been installed, like a locked door that could not be opened. It was done deliberately…I could feel it. But by who? This was very frustrating to say the least. I was being allowed to know what someone wanted me to know…that's what it felt like.

I 'spoke' to my father, and I wished that he could hear me. I sent thoughts to him that I was here inside his mind trying to access a part of it, hoping that he would respond, but I knew that he would not. I was a virtual image in his real image world. I did not exist, and he could not sense me, yet I could sense him, and I knew that I could influence him. I cannot explain the processing of my thoughts to achieve this, other than comparing it to a conscious and a subconscious mind. I could do things behind the scenes so to speak in his subconscious that would influence his conscious…and it would just happen. There was no A to B to C…it just took place. But I knew that there was something missing that I needed to find out before I committed to my planned actions. There was something I should know that was being held from me. I cannot explain that either. It was just an inner feeling of knowing…or should I say of NOT knowing.

My father slept at the base. He had his own private quarters and very nice it was too. Not as sophisticated and futuristic as my dome of course, but nice and comfortable, and he seemed to be 'high up' in the pecking order. Any base personnel walking past him would salute and look for his recognition of them. It made me feel proud of him and I was pleased that he was held in such high esteem. I just wish though that I didn't have these nagging doubts in my head about his true feelings. I really could not see how he would change his views and go to the American government after the assassination with his knowledge. His thoughts towards the deed seemed so strong and dedicated. Like I said earlier, he would need to do a complete U-turn!

Was it the guilt afterwards or perhaps for the safety of me and mum that he lied and made up a story, because he knew that he would spend the rest of his life looking over his shoulder?

I decided I needed to see this so-called document that was going to change everything so much. And why had he kept it and not destroyed it? Perhaps that was the part I was overlooking, and that he did have a deep rooted plan that he was going to instigate. Mind you, nothing had come to light in 'my normal time' as far as I was aware, and how could he possibly know that one day I would mind-travel back in time to influence him to do something with it?

My goodness, I had so much going around in my head it was hard to think straight myself!

We were sitting at the head of a long table situated in a large room that was lit by multiple fluorescent tubes which were hanging in metal boxes from the rather high ceiling. My father was in charge, I could feel his sense of power and authority. I really wish I could read his mind properly, but all I could understand were his feelings. It frustrates me as I know a year or two ago I could probably have done so, but then again I guess I wouldn't have been able to be doing what I'm doing now.

My father checked his tie with his hand, stood up, then began to speak.

"Good morning gentlemen...I wanted to get us all together today as I needed to update you on a few developments at the base."

He looked at the ten faces around the table, five on each side. Don was closest on our left with four men in white lab coats sitting alongside him. Opposite them were four men of military stature and then there was another man who was sitting at the end. He had slicked back hair and was wearing a black waistcoat and a buttoned up to the neck white shirt, and my father's gaze lingered on him for a few moments until the man turned his head and our eyes met...

Oh my god...it was DANNY...I'm sure of it!

It felt like he was looking through my father's eyes and directly INTO mine.

It was him!

I couldn't believe it!

I'm sure it was him!

I was trying to fathom out how this could be, as my father began...

"Now, I know you're all aware of the mounting concern that is plaguing our existence here...and I want to reassure you immediately that the importance of our work totally outweighs any outside interference, and that matters are in hand to reduce the threat accordingly. That's all I am at liberty to say on the subject, but please be confident that our time and tasks here will not be jeopardised."

My father paused, and I could feel the seriousness and commitment in his mind as he looked at the slowly nodding heads.

I could sense the strength in his belief and I could see the respect in their faces and the command-like effect he had on them. He was very unusually direct with his words, but again, what he was saying seemed to be implying that he was very much for the assassination. They didn't know that he was talking about that of course, but I did. Well, I think I did, unless there was something else that was being planned, but I was looking for any excuse in my mind to NOT implicate my father.

The meeting lasted for another 10 minutes or so during which time the awareness of Danny being there to my father came over as very strong, though I felt a nervousness and reservation which I could not comprehend. And above all, it WAS Danny, I know it, which totally floored me. His voice was the same but his manner and persona were completely different. He spoke 'older' and 'wiser' almost authoritative-like and had a complete air of calmness.

He was the first to excuse himself at the end of the meeting and leave the room, and immediately I felt a slightly more relaxed feeling with my father.

I could also detect an ease in the atmosphere with the other's too as they all looked towards us.

"The boys seem to be improving," said my father in a thankful and reassuring tone to which everyone responded approvingly.

"It's been a difficult and worrying time I know, and I appreciate you and your respective teams for the effort in all aspects of their care and with ongoing relationships…"

My father paused, and I could feel great discernment and apprehension, yet I sensed a submission and acceptance to the whole situation. I felt frustrated as I could not determine the reasoning for these thoughts. I knew though, that the 'boys' were extra-terrestrials and that made me feel really excited with the wonder and amazement of it all, yet I also felt worried and concerned. This was very serious stuff that my father was involved in.

"I'm sure you're feeling a lot happier and relieved too, Bernie," said one of the uniformed men with a smile... "It must be a really strange situation for you to be in...an emotional one too."

My father slowly nodded his head, then exhaled and smiled as he engaged eye contact.

"You're right John...it is...and let's hope that I've done the right thing...that WE...have done the right thing!"

The significance of the situation was overpowering. I could feel the anxiety in my father yet there was a great caring concern too. A feeling that was warm with hope and trust. It was good to feel that but I could not understand it. My father had agreed to something or had done something, but I did not know what. And why do they keep calling him Bernie?

I wanted to learn more from my father. Find out what he was really doing and what he had already done. As I mentioned, I felt so frustrated that I could not delve deeper to another level in his mind and more so now regarding Danny. Would I be able to do that in the future again as I got older? I've no idea. But at the moment it was really annoying that I could not. Because right now I was 'looking' and 'hearing' and relying on his surface feelings and his simple thoughts, and the picture that they were painting did not put him in a good light. Perhaps I could influence him to be different. Perhaps that's what I did and he became the man that I thought I knew. But I cannot change the past can I? Who really knows for sure. But I know what the 'future' holds, and I'm just here to complete the attachment and to make the 'futures' future a better and honest place. I must keep that in MY mind and stop thinking too much. I was turning him into some kind of mad and evil scientist who was trying to destroy the world. Far from it of course, but I cannot stop thinking that I didn't really know him. All my life, right up until he died, I always thought that there was another side to him; that there was a part of him that I never knew about. And that thought has been reinforced with later comments from my mother along with different happenings that we experienced and of course all his involvement with Time City and the Hub…and ALL THIS!

And now Danny is here in the 60s looking the same as he did in the 80s!

I've got to get a grip with it all.

That evening my father was working alone, sitting behind the large dark oak desk in his office. I had 'switched' myself back on to focus and observe. Now was a good time to try out the influence and to see that document. I mindfully focused and suggested we go to the safe, get the paper, and bring it back to the desk. He dutifully responded and pulled the document out of the envelope and moved the desk lamp accordingly to highlight the wording, and then 'we' began to read.

He wanted to scan, but I wanted to read as much as I could, and I focused on him reading all the words.

I tried to understand what had been written, but so much of it did not make any sense to me.

It was a series of authoritative instructions all seemingly related to retaining secrecy of operations at the base. There was a cover letter that read:

'*In the context of the above it has become necessary to review and evaluate duplication of field activities in light of the current situation. To eliminate this problem, I have drafted new directives for your review and consideration.*

Please evaluate each draft on its own merit with the goal of finding acceptable solutions in which we all can agree on. As you must know LANCER has made some inquiries regarding our activities which we cannot allow. Please submit your views no later than October. Your action to this matter is critical to the continuance of the group.'

I influenced my father to read through each directive which he did and I could feel him paying particular attention to one that was entitled 'Project Environment.'…and part of this read:

'*When conditions become non-conducive for growth in our environment and Washington cannot be influenced any further, the weather is lacking any precipitation…it should be wet.*'

Again, this made absolutely no sense to me. The language was so uncertain and obscure, but I could feel my father responding to the wording.

I let my 'influence' drop slightly and 'watched' as my father continued to digest the print. It meant something to him for sure. And who was LANCER?

Knowing what I know from the 'future', I would say that that is probably a code name for the president. He was investigating and perhaps trying to infiltrate operations and gain total influence, and the way that it is written indicates that it was obviously affecting them all in the negative sense.

So my father was being asked to agree or disagree to these directives and these instructions were trying to prevent the president from obtaining control, in any way or form, of the operations and activities which were taking place at the base, and that obviously included these extra-terrestrial 'boys.' How did we obtain them and what was the plan to do with them? If there is a plan! There really couldn't have been one that involved public knowledge as I knew nothing of any of this in 'present' time and that was over twenty years away. But if the president did take control, it would mean exposing these 'secrets' which would inform the world once and for all that 'we are not alone.' There's obviously a lot more that I do not know, but the extra-terrestrial presence, if broadcast to the world, would change things wouldn't it? And for the better or for the worse?

I 'switched off' from my father and started to think more. How would the world's people react if they knew that aliens were living on the planet with them? And the big question would be…WHY?

People would feel agitated, worried and threatened. Why had they not been told before? Is there a secret agenda? There could be a total law and order breakdown…It could turn the whole world into turmoil!

I started to think about what one of the president's aides had said; that the world was being lied to, that there was incredible technology and power and amazing life changing medicine already available that would revolutionise the planet. It was already here 'now,' courtesy of our 'visitors,' but it was apparently being held back from us by this so-called self-governing state that sat out here in the Nevada desert; this secret state that was a law unto itself…of which my father was part of!

I was thinking much too much again, but I needed to know that what I was going to do was correct for all and sundry. There were two sides to this, and I could understand the reasoning of both…but the assassination of a president to fulfil one's aims is taking it too far. But I could not see anything in any of the directives that suggested that the president should be actually killed to achieve it, unless the obscure wording was a code or had a special meaning that only my father and his colleagues understood. It certainly said that the president needed to be prevented from infiltrating the organisation, and the directives put forward for my father and his cronies to peruse were really just obstacles to slow down the president, to put him off, hoping that he would lose interest and move onto other matters…

My father put a paper clip over the corner of the sheets of paper and pushed them back into the envelope and returned the documents to the safe. Then he walked to the front of his desk and stopped, turned, and looked into the wall mirror. He was side-on to it and made efforts to correct his body position so that he was looking directly at it…then he moved closer…

I felt really odd. I was 'looking' right into his eyes. Does he know I'm here? Of course he doesn't!

He kept staring, and then he adjusted his tie, wriggling it from side to side, and pushing it up further.

He smiled…It was like he was smiling at ME!

Oh my goodness…he DOES know I'm here! But surely it's not possible.

"DAD, IT'S ME...JAMIE...I'M HERE!" I was 'shouting'...reacting to the sudden realisation...

Then his expression changed and his hand suddenly went up to his face and he scratched the side of his nose with a fingernail as he moved forward, then he examined the pointed finger and immediately looked back to the mirror and moved closer towards it again to view...a pimple.

I stopped 'shouting'...

It was ridiculous of me to even THINK that he knew I was here.

But for a moment...it was a real feeling, and it felt so good. He was really with me, really looking at me...

And I realised how much I loved him...

After another 5 minutes or so he cleared and packed up his work from the desk and we made our way back to his quarters where he poured himself out a coffee from the percolator and made a sandwich.

When he sat down to eat and relax I 'switched off' from him completely and thought some more.

He was going back home to Dallas next week for a few days and that was the planned moment of opportunity to influence him regarding taking the documents to a lawyer. That gives me 4 or 5 days beforehand of 'sitting around' in my father's mind, observing, listening, thinking and hopefully learning more about the whole situation here. I know my goal is to complete the attachment instructions, but I wanted to know more about my father's part in all this. I was still unsure about so many things. Dr Bradshaw said that my father didn't have time to alert the government of the assassination intentions. But I realise now that he must have had a couple of weeks in hand if he really did want to inform, though at the moment his feelings were far from it.

I started to wonder what today's date actually was as I 'switched' back on, and immediately I could hear music playing. Sounds were emanating from a rather large radiogram situated against the wall and my father was nodding his head in appreciation of the dance beat. I influenced and suggested another coffee and my father got up and walked into the kitchen. I knew that there was a red and white numerical calendar on one of the cupboard doors and I influenced him to take a look.

Thursday 29 June…1961!

WHAT? The assassination took place on the 22nd of November…1963!

My father went back over to the coffee percolator and refilled his cup…

Oh my goodness, forget a 'few weeks in hand', he knew YEARS in advance of the assassination! It wasn't just a last minute episode like Dr Bradshaw had portrayed. He actually had all the time in the world to bring it to the attention of the United States government…if he wanted to!

"DAD!" I said 'out loud'…"What are you doing?"

This was SO frustrating. As I found out more information, the more doubts I had in my mind about the whole situation. And let's not forget that there was nothing written directly in the directives anyway that point blank asked for my father's vote to assassinate President Kennedy, although I must be honest the thought 'patterns' I can feel from him do indicate a strong desire to 'stop' JFK.

What altered his beliefs over the next 2 years or so? Something must have happened and he 'came to his senses' and then went to the government with his story. That must be it. But what? I needed to know, but I'm in the wrong time frame to find out. And I'm certainly not going to 'hang around' for two years!

Could I instigate a jaunt within a jaunt?

I have thought about it now and then whether it was possible, and I do know that I have experienced it anyway years ago. But at the time it was totally out of my control, and I put it down to a 'growing up' episode, like my version of going through adolescence.

But if I could do it and I could jaunt close to just before November 22nd 1963, I could see what actual state of mind my father was in. It would tell me once and for all whether he did do a U-turn or not, and if he did, hopefully it would explain why!

I so wanted to know this, and my feelings to fully complete the attachment to the requirements were waning due to all the doubts in my mind as to whether I was actually doing the right thing. I needed more information and jaunting nearer to the assassination date would certainly give me more.

But could I do it? I've never been able to specify a time and date before, hence the 'Hub' and the 'Bubble.'…and now, on reflection, it seems that they were wildly out…or were they? I'm only here to get the directive document so I guess they were right. I just had it in my mind that it would be a couple of days away from the assassination, not a couple of YEARS…especially after what Dr Bradshaw had said.

I know I wanted to go back to when I was very young once…and it worked, but it was 'potluck' really. I do not know the full mind operation needed to actually achieve the specifics, but I do know now that I can jaunt when I want to, so hopefully if I concentrate on what I want…it will happen.

I have to give it a go.

I can't move forward until I know my father's true motives and outcome in all this. I've never felt so indecisive about something so important. If my father was not involved, it would be much simpler. But I've learnt so much here too, and my mindset now is quite different to how it was when I arrived.

I 'switched off' and focused…

I'm going to do it now…

I know I can do it…and I have to do it.

I closed my 'eyes'…

I saw the blackness…the opening…and I was through…

Explanatory Thoughts

I opened my eyes.

I'm not in my father's mind!

Where am I?

I'm lying in a bed, propped up on pillows.

I moved my head to look around, feeling stiff resistance in my neck as I blinked a few times to focus.

There was a small sidelight sitting on a dressing table to my left that softly lit the room and to my right there was an illuminated hospital type medical monitor which was quietly beeping. I noticed two or three tubes extending from it, and I instinctively raised my arm realising that they were probably attached to me…and they were, at my wrist and my leg. There was a quiet whirring sound coming from some kind of metal box unit in the corner of the room which was expelling cool air towards me.

I looked at the door immediately in front, which was slightly open exposing stronger light from within.

I could hear someone moving around.

I swallowed then tried to speak.

My mouth felt really dry.

"Hello?" I said in a feeble, quiet, croaky voice...it was almost a whisper...I swallowed again. "Hello," I repeated slightly louder.

The noise stopped outside the door and then I could hear footsteps.

Suddenly, the door was pushed back and a bespectacled blonde haired woman, with eyes wide and mouth open, hurried towards me.

Was it Anna? Yes, she looked different but yes, it was Anna!

"Jamie! Oh my god...you're back, you're back...I don't believe it!"

I felt really good at seeing her again, but totally bewildered as to the situation.

"What...what's going on?" I asked in a stumbling perplexed tone as my lips tried to form the words.

"Don't try to speak...just take it easy...OH MY GOD, I can't believe it. I'm so pleased you've come back...I knew you would!"

I coughed, the weakest cough imaginable, slowly blinked, and then looked at her happy smiling face as she gently held my arm with both her hands.

It started to dawn on me what might have happened...

"Don't worry...I've been here looking after you...oh wow, this is awesome...I'll go and get you some water, hold on, I'll be right back..."

She turned and practically ran out of the room before I could say anything...and I started to think...

...I must be in the hospital section again of Time City, though it doesn't feel like a medical room. A few hours must have passed instead of the forecast minutes...and wow, Dr

Maskell was right, the chair certainly takes it out of you, I felt whacked.

"There you go!" said Anna as she bustled back in. She caringly held the mug up to my mouth, but I took it from her hand.

"Now sip it slowly...don't rush," she responded.

The water tasted like nectar to my dry tongue and I struggled not to gulp...

"Anna...tell me...what's happened?...how long have I been away?" I slowly asked in between sips.

"It's about three years now. We moved you back..."

"THREE YEARS!" I interrupted with a cough and splutter... "Moved me back? Moved me back where?"

"We moved you back here about six months ago and..."

"Move me back where?" I interrupted again.

"To the UK...England...you're back in your lovely house..." she declared as she held her hands out as if introducing me to the place.

I looked around again, slowly rolling my head on the pillow.

"I knew this day would come...I just knew it!" she continued excitedly.

I didn't know what to say. I was so mixed with my feelings, though the fact that I hadn't completed the attachment successfully was in the forefront of my mind.

I was back in my own time, albeit I had lost a LOT of it somehow.

THREE years! that's ridiculous...it's impossible, it cannot be three years!

As I tried to understand what had happened I could feel my body rejuvenating. Strength was returning to my arms and legs. My neck was becoming supple; my eyes felt more lubricated and focused as I looked at my hands and began flexing my fingers. It was like I had been injected with some special energy boosting serum that was rapidly circulating my body.

"You've hardly had any muscle wastage, Jamie…it's remarkable…and your hair hasn't grown," she excitedly said as she watched me 'warming up.' "…and look, you've got no facial hair growth either," she exclaimed as she softly held my chin… "It's amazing."

I smiled and looked at her. She conveyed so much warmth and kindness; her eyes sparkled as her soft gaze encompassed my eyes with a comforting glow of affection. Her face was beautiful. I'd always known that, and the realisation of her wonder was hitting home again.

The THREE lost years were definitely hitting home too…

"You'd better fill me in on what's happened since I've been away…and Anna…"

I paused as I looked at her and smiled… "Thank you for what you've done…have you seriously been with me all the time?"

She leant forward and kissed me on the cheek, "of course I have…and I feel like I'm practically British now," she said as she laughed and then held my hand…

I must be honest; I was taken aback by her strong affection towards me. I knew we always had a connection, but she had never been like this, and besides, it had all ended rather abruptly in Time City without even a goodbye.

"…I love it here," she continued, "It's so quiet and so peaceful. I never thought I'd say that being a Dallas girl, but it's true…especially after the craziness in the world that followed your attachment escapade! You had them all as mad as hell there you know, until they finally found it."

I had no idea what she was going on about, but I had a feeling that I should not confess to anything at the moment and just 'go along' with what she was saying…

"Oh dear, were they not amused then?" I asked with a big grin on my face as if I knew that I'd done something that I shouldn't have…

She spent the next ten minutes or so informing me of what had taken place…

A letter, not documents, was delivered to the President of the United States on the given arranged day and time. It contained geographical coordinates and a single word, 'BURIED.' The coordinates led them to a bank of grass in Dealey Plaza, Dallas. The government, using a ground penetrating detection system, located three possible targets and commenced exploration. Two were false trails, but one was a container that held the wanted documents…that has 'changed the world'.

The secret base known as S4 in the Nevada desert, and other secret bases around the globe, have been invaded by the relevant governments. Every one of them has been exposed for housing extra-terrestrial life forms with evidence of human/alien breeding programmes with integration of the offspring into Earth's society. The planet is now a very nervous, untrusting and worrying place to live. The age old question of 'Are we alone?' has been answered and there is a new question on everyone's lips… 'Why are they here?'

The fear of an actual invasion by some far away space force is on everyone's mind even though the WGB (World Governing Body) has assured the Earth's people that it will

222

not happen. And how do they know this? Because apparently communication has been going on for many years between alien species and the secret 'governing' societies, and the new governments say that if an invasion was going to take place, it most certainly would have already happened by now.

But there is a huge concern that the WGB is not just composed of humans. It is said that alien entities are now very much a part of the mechanism and are overseeing, and to a certain extent controlling, the day to day decision making and management of the planet…and people are rightly scared and worried for the future.

"We know too much now, Jamie…and too much information has also led to speculation and rumours about the true purpose of the human race."

I was looking deep into Anna's eyes. She had not let go of my hand and was caressing and rubbing it as she spoke.

"The true purpose?" I queried, "What do you mean?"

She hesitated, and then spoke…

"It is said that we are just an experimental race…that the world is one big laboratory, where scientists are studying our evolution…"

"What scientists?" I asked.

"Exactly, Jamie…exactly!"

She leant further forward and kissed my hand.

"Oh I'm sorry," she said smiling nervously. "I'm just so pleased that you're back with me…but I'm sure you'll wish you'd never have gone through with it all when you actually see and experience the big picture for yourself."

My mind was working overtime…

I knew that I had not completed the attachment, so it wasn't me that had influenced my father to deliver the letter and bury the documents. So he must have done that on his own accord. But the chances of him doing that, and arranging the date of delivery etc that coincided with my attachment instructions…well, that was nigh on impossible…it just couldn't have happened!

The Time City people must have somehow detected that I had big doubts about completing the attachment.

Perhaps the chair and the bubble could 'read' my thoughts or even 'see' what I was doing? That must be it, and they had a plan B ready to swing into action and they kept me 'away' until they got everything organised for someone else to carry out the attachment?

It was naive of me to even think that they would put all their eggs in one basket. There must be others with my abilities awaiting the call up.

Was one of them Danny? There is much in my mind that says all this revolves around him. Has he been 'working' for them all along? Is he a true time traveller?

It's all unclear and not making sense at the moment but I could feel the remaining 'powers' entering my mind, like the last gushes of water from a tap that was filling a barrel.

It was surging into me, and I knew I was almost up to the brim.

I sat up, pushed the sheet back and removed the monitoring equipment from my body.

"Jamie!" exclaimed Anna.

"No, it's alright…I'm fine." I swung my legs off the bed and onto the floor.

She let go of my hand and took a step back.

"Be careful…you might fall."

I wouldn't…I knew I wouldn't.

I could feel the strength in my muscles, in my body, in my legs…AND in my mind!

My brain was altering, strengthening, expanding…I could feel it happening…and it was taking place at an incredibly fast rate!

I stood up as Anna regained her grip on my hand.

I grinned, "Anyone would think you really cared for me…"

She shied away…then looked back…

"Well, I hope you still feel the same about me after all this time," she said smiling as she lifted her hand, advertising the ring on her finger.

I reacted immediately with a look of horror then smiled and squeezed her hand.

My response was well acted.

"What's the time, and where are we? I don't recognise this room at all," I said as I pointed to the huge TV screen on the wall with an expression of bewilderment but with a memory of knowing.

Anna went over to the patio windows and pulled back the curtains and the net curtains beneath, exposing a deep orange ball of light that was peeping up over the horizon.

"It's the start of a new day, Jamie," she announced. "…and this is our new bedroom…well, when I say new, it's been here for a year now. I had the room converted so that when you returned, you could wake up to this lovely view each morning…and you have…and you can…"

Her voice was slightly quivering and I could see her eyes were glassy and watery.

"Come here," I said as I moved towards her, taking hold of her arms, and pulling her close.

225

As we hugged I became aware again of the growing force within my mind. An energy that was building, forming and creating. I was also aware of an intermittent humming sound; a resonance deep inside my head. I knew it was almost time…

"I'm sorry Jamie, it's been so long. I'm just so glad you're here…"

I mentally refocused…and kissed her lips, then leaned back as I looked at her, exaggerating my stare.

"By the way, I love the specs and the new blonde hair style. It's a lot more wavy…AND you've lost your fringe."

Anna looked at me with a slightly perplexed expression. "…Have you been seeing someone else whilst you've been away?" she mockingly asked. Then she laughed and slid open the patio doors and beckoned me outside. The heat hit me immediately as we walked across the patio and then stood together, taking in the amazing view that lay before us as the hot sun began its early morning climb into the awakening sky. I felt the heat from the gentle breeze against my skin as sounds of bird song broke the calming silence. I took a deep breath and satisfyingly exhaled. It was so good to be back on English soil, though I looked down at what was actually beneath my bare feet… "It's artificial grass," said Anna reacting to the scripted puzzled look on my face as she entwined her arm closer with mine. "It has to be that now if you want to see something green."

"It's all the rage in Dallas, don't you know," she added in her attempt at a posh English accent.

I smiled.

"Is it just you and me here?" I asked knowingly.

"Yeah," she replied, "just you and me." They used to phone every day at the beginning, to check. Then it became once a week, once every two. Now it's been left up to me to make contact when you return.

"They thought that you'd been 'away' far too long…that something had gone wrong with your mind mechanics."

"My mind mechanics?" I queried.

"I know," replied Anna smiling, "that's what they call it."

"Oh…so they've given up on me, have they?" I said.

She smiled and slowly shook her head disapprovingly…

"So much has changed, Jamie. It's like we're living in a science fiction movie, it really is…the world is a completely different place now."

I could feel more processes taking place in my mind as I looked deep into her eyes…

"What colour is my toothbrush?"

"I'm sorry?" she said in a surprised tone.

I smiled, paused and kept looking into her eyes…

"No, don't worry, it's OK…I'm just thinking out loud…"

I paused again as she continued to stare at me…

"Tell me what happened at the Hub when I never 'returned'…what did you all do?"

She hesitated for a few moments…her facial expression was one of thoughtful confusion.

I smiled, "come on, tell me…what happened?"

Anna's eyes were unblinking as if trying to reach inside my mind.

It was probably just as well that she did not have the ability to do so!

"OK…" she said enthusiastically as her thoughts switched back… "One minute you're going on the attachment, the next minute we hear that the letter has been delivered. We knew that was how it was going to be, but it was still really strange when it actually took place. Then we kept monitoring you, waiting for you to return, and after about an hour we moved you from the bubble to the hospital section."

I grinned, "That must have been stunning TV viewing for the president."

Anna smiled…then reacted as if she suddenly remembered something…

"Let's go back inside. I've got something to give to you."

We walked back through the 'new' bedroom and into the living room where she opened my bureau and turned to face me with a sealed envelope in her hand.

"It's from the president, Jamie. I was instructed to give this to you when you came back."

I looked into Anna's eyes then down at the official looking letter as I took it from her, opened it and began to read…

Dear Jamie,

The world thanks you. Through your amazing abilities and efforts, you have opened the gate to the pathway of truth, and the world's inhabitants are now aware. The direction is daunting, but we must be positive and ride this course with unwavering courage to ensure the continuance of mankind.

The greater our knowledge increases, the more our ignorance unfolds. But we must not forget that to know is to understand and with understanding we recommence our existence, for every accomplishment starts with the decision to try.

I must also thank you for allowing the reality of Jacqueline's demise to be finally exposed. We can never bring her back, but justice has been served and years of speculation and anxiety for me and my family can be truly put to rest.

For this I am eternally grateful.

Sincerely yours,
John F Kennedy

As I read the words and the president's name, a light to my life's meaning suddenly shone brightly like a new-born star.

Images of past, present and future instantaneously ran through my brain in a final psychedelic bombardment of inter-dimensional data. Meandering processes and wandering thoughts were now honed with direction. I had a total understanding...of everything!

I suddenly felt incredibly powerful.

I lowered the letter and looked up at Anna.

"I need to tell you a few more things…" she said smiling, though I could see that it was tinged with nervousness…and I knew why.

I also knew that the colour of my toothbrush was most definitely not blue!

My father was right.

The mind IS the universe…MY mind is the universe!

All that matters within multi-dimensional space and time…is right here and now!

The hum in my brain was constant.

I am complete.

I blinked and mentally focused as she continued…

"There were a lot of things that took place in Time City that I didn't agree with but I had to comply…and I was taken off your assignment because of that."

"Assignment? You make me sound like I was allocated to you as a job!" I consciously exclaimed as I calmly put down the letter, took hold of her hand, and guided her back through the house.

She looked at me cautiously a few times as I led her through the doorway and onto the patio where we stopped walking and I turned to face her as she began to speak…

"I'm sorry, Jamie…you were a task that was given to us at the time and we all fell in line behind the directives…I just didn't realise that I'd fall in love as well. I was so thrilled when we got engaged, but when you said you were going into battle, it scared me…you gave me the impression that you might not return."

I looked at her.

This lovely woman…THIS lovely Anna.

From the first moment we had met, I was attracted to her and I always wanted her to feel the same way.

She seemed special and I can sense the innermost feelings that I had in that time and space…

But Jane had always said to me. "Never let your heart rule your head", so how ironic it was that my true mother allowed it to happen to her.

She went against strict protocol because of the way Kai was maturing. She took risks for my advancement and wellbeing, and assisted in the installation of the needed knowledge and abilities throughout my life. She protected me from, and showed me, the forces that do not want my kind to progress. She influenced me to assist others because she knew that I would develop in the way that they wanted. Her understanding of the part that I was to play in her time and dimension was paramount to her actions. And though she attempted to intervene occasionally in the very unforeseen immoral development of Kai, the magnitude of the importance of her non-involvement in the arrangement was too strong to abuse, and so, she continued to observe…like Dan.

Guiding Steve from an early misfortune and experiencing him in his life dimension is satisfying.

Knowing that my other brother Kai 'influenced' me wrongly from his…is not!

But I am now ready…

…and they know.

I gave Anna a kiss, pulled her close and we hugged…because that is what she wanted.

"I'm not going to tell them that you're back...not yet," she said. "If I do, things will change again...and I don't want that. I want us to always be like this."

I smiled and knowingly looked across the valley; my line of sight resting on the equilibrium, majesty and significance of the white house.

I immediately entered.

"Are you alright?"

Anna's voice refocused me...

I returned and sent a command to Max, then replied,

"I couldn't be any better..."

The End

Ingram Content Group UK Ltd.
Milton Keynes UK
UKHW020638220623
423865UK00011B/595